SALLY ASHTON

Sally Ashton grew up in Yorkshire and from the age of fifteen has been involved with the Writing Squad (An Arts Council initiative for young Northern writers). She studied Creative Writing at the University of Warwick and last year finished a Master's in Translation and Interpreting in London. In between her degrees she travelled extensively and spent time working in France, Canada, Spain and Austria. She currently lives in Berlin, working as a translator. In her spare time she loves playing sport, reading and drinking a lot of coffee.

Controller was shortlisted for the Route Next Great Author Award and shortlisted for best novella in the Sabotage Review Awards 2013.

DEAD INK

CONTROLLER
SALLY ASHTON

DEAD INK

First published in Great Britain in 2014 by Dead Ink

An imprint of Cinder House

42 Seedley Park Road, Salford. Greater Manchester. M6 5NT

ISBN 978-0-9576985-8-1

Edited by Wes Brown

Cover art by Estelle Morris

WWW.DEADINKBOOKS.COM

WWW.CINDERHOUSE.COM

For Danny, Steve and Mrs Todd

Authors note

This book started taking shape as I was finishing university and was an exploration of the Male Gaze and women's reaction under it. The publication coincided with a rise in popularity of erotica and, while I never intended it to be interpreted as such, it has been a lesson for me in accepting that an audience will not interpret your work as you necessarily intend.

I go inside the café and I speak with a woman this time. She is all happy and round-soft edges. I tell her that I am here to model and her smiles become even larger. She is very gentle with me, as though she is handling a live dove.

Pienso que nadie esta aquí pero…espera cinco minutos y pienso que los estudiantes lleguen.

But there is a man in a corner.

Sí, sí. Drags out the sound, the e sound. Nodding. Handling and stroking my feathers.

Un hombre, sí. El espera. Always he is… – she pauses. Clicks her tongue…*aquí para este clase.*

I sit and wait, picking up an art book that I cannot read. The words fall off the page in front of me. I look at the pictures.

I cannot concentrate. Aware of my thighs beside each other. Sweat making them sticky as I sit, waiting.

I feel that sick feeling again. The sweat is beginning to make little pools on me. I touch my inner arms. Feel the soft, wet pit. I think that she said that I should wait, that the students should arrive soon, but I don't know.

Stand up and replace the book. I try to read the other titles but the mixtures of letters fall out of my sight and onto the painted floorboards. I reach a gap in the bookshelf. In the space there is a plant. Its tendrils spill down over the shelf. I lean close to the plant and shut my eyes. It smells like the colour green. The plant has no flowers. Thick, smooth leaves. Fat and identical. I can still picture them behind my closed eyes. I stand there, blind, still and smelling. Sweat heavy trickling from my armpits, cold and slow down the sides of my body. Blind, still, and smelling the colour green.

I open my eyes. The man in the corner is looking at me. I have been shut-eyed for minutes perhaps, but the smiling woman has not even raised her head from her counter. He watches me. I watch him watch. I think that he is not looking into my eyes but further down. He could see part of me through the shelf below. I feel a sweat patch from my legs blotted on my dress. I imagine the soft, downy hair on my legs. Regard him for a moment. His eyes do not falter. They are very clear, even from this distance. I blink and I move. I move sideways until I cannot see him and my waist cannot see him. I try and read the book titles but still nothing. My language is disintegrating before my eyes, but nobody notices because I am foreign here. I am pale and grey, not like the dark-haired and dark-eyed Spanish girls with their short fringes and rich skin. I stand out.

The man from the corner stands up, leaving his file and bag on the table. It is still so hot in here. He talks to the smiling Spanish woman and she looks at me and then she looks at him. Then she walks over, bringing her soft and large smile. *Empezamos?* I nod.

When I stand up she is very small beside me. She walks to the man and picks up his file and bag. He stands and does not thank her for her help. His left arm is slightly in front of him, the shoulder a soft hunch, the hand hanging loosely near her face as she leans down. It waves gently, as though in a breeze. She does not react to it hovering beside her cheek whilst she picks up the file. I let him walk ahead of me so that I can watch his arm. He does not carry anything with it. Instead the limb moves of its own accord, gentle and retarded. Fingers soft splay, light in between them, empty hand. I wonder how he will draw with this disability. I wonder if I will look ugly in his drawings because of his ugly arm. We follow her up the stairs and she points out the bathroom to me. She points out the art room at the end of hallway. It dazzles with light.

I am in the toilet and I take off all of my clothes. They are damp. I am sick a little, finally, into the toilet. I look at myself in the mirror for a while. Wipe vomit from my lips. My lips are vomity little lines.

The man is sitting on the chair that is closest to the raised wooden platform and the smiling woman is adjusting his easel. He sits and directs her. He is slow and gentle as he opens his bag. He uses only his right hand. He takes a smaller bag onto his lap and from this takes charcoals one by one. Carefully. Handling each one with a pinch of forefinger and thumb. Placing the brittle sticks on the ledge of the easel. I see the black dust that they leave on his

2

fingers. When the woman is finished with his arrangements, she comes towards me. Her face carries the light from the room with it, like a sun. She stops in front of me, puts her hand on my arm. Smile so wide. Then turns, goes. Hear her feet on the steps. I look back. I watch the light follow her along the dark hall, make out the pictures on the walls. Turn. I watch the man while he arranges himself. Just him and me. His right arm is working and arranging, tense and careful over what it touches. His left arm is in front of him, to the side, relaxed, waving, as though conducting some sound that only it can hear.

I stand on the slightly raised platform. The man looks at me. The lights look at me. The man's face is expectant, but also calm. I look back at him as I stand there. My gown is on the floor. My lower stomach feels vulnerable, my upper thighs pale and sensitive. I wait for him to say something because I don't know what to do. He speaks, eventually. *Pose and hold. I'll time 5 minutes.* Puts his eyes back down. *I'll tell you when to stop.* He speaks English. I understand it, not like the Spanish that was falling off the pages of the art books. I hold my arms out and drop one leg. I have been practicing posing in the mirror. I am obedient and still, a good girl. The look on his face hardens, his eyes flick between the paper and me. Can hear the sound of the charcoal. I watch him and his arm, the useless arm that doesn't care about drawing. I feel drops of sweat blooming on my chest under the light. I blink and his eyes do not catch mine again. Hear a sound on the steps. There are two people, embarrassed for being late. I do not turn to look at them. I keep still.

I change my pose frequently. For an hour I furl, stretch and expose my bones, move my hair from my back, lift a foot, wince as the pressure from kneeling burns in my joints. As more and more people arrive, I turn my poses so that my back is to the man who was first here. He is the only person who speaks, directing the type of pose that he would like next. His voice stands out in the silence of the room. I obey him. He says nothing as I turn, pose by pose, from facing him to the other direction to facing him again. The lights heat me. I feel eyes staring at me. Dampness on my thighs. My cold toes. His eyes drawing me. My ribs cutting a little through my skin.

3

W e have a break. I walk, half-wrapped in my gown, to the bathroom. I wait, leaning on the edge of the sink, until somebody bangs on the door. A woman.

I look down at her whilst she moves past me and forces me to move back into the hallway as she shuts the door to the bathroom. I walk around, looking at their drawings. A young woman begins to talk to me. She has remained in her seat and looks up at me, eyes wide, smile flicking up and down whilst she points, fluttering fingers, at her pictures. I smile down and nod whilst she moves from one sketch to the next. She has left a smudge for my face in every picture apart from the last. Here, she explains my jagged chin and nose and cheekbone, my hair a long black mark. Her Spanish is caught in my ears so that I cannot reply often because I do not understand her. She gradually blushes at my silence and quickens in her movement and speech. Looks at my stomach which is at eye-level from where she sits. I move on whilst she is still embarrassed and explaining herself. I look at the other drawings but they are the same lines, the same uncaught angles. Everyone concentrates on a different aspect of the body. Some on faces, some on bones that stick out of paper skin, and some draw plump flesh hanging limp off bones. *De donde eres? Obviamente no eres de aquí, no?* A young man begins to speak to me in Spanish but then changes into broken English. *Nunca te he visto aquí, trabajas mucho de modelo, working?* Smiling at me, he points to the lines and shapes that he has made. He says the word model with strange Spanish vowels. Smile back and shuffle my feet, looking around whilst he talks. The lights in the room are shiny, sweaty. He is still speaking. I open my gown a little and I watch him stare at the line of skin that I reveal down my side, a strip of waist and hip. He continues to talk whilst looking. When I cover the skin, his eyes try to find mine again, but they cannot. His face flushes red. I return to the raised platform. The small step makes the nausea flair up inside me. I am facing the wooden back of the man's easel. His returning steps break the silence of the ugly lines that the others are carving. His left hand waves towards me. He doesn't look at me at all but puts down his coffee and arranges himself, the hand still wafting.

I am confused by it.

We are tired, him and I. He looks at his subject finally, brow furrowed. I watch him. Soon he tells me to pose again. His eyes follow the lines of all parts of my body, not just one dissected part. Tired. Vomit taste. The class is over soon.

Hablando del clase. Sometimes their eyes and smiles miss mine, and sometimes they turn underneath mine as I look directly into their faces. Hands paw nervously at their new files and heavy leaves of paper. I leave quickly. Don't want to sit alone among them. The nervous girl who tried to explain her work to me waves, saying *Adiós*. The young man who spoke in broken English to me says goodbye but I do not reply.

The man is waiting outside the doorway. There is a light shower of rain. The air is being washed clean. I breathe, a sudden hunger for fresh air. I don't feel sick anymore.

Stop.

I stop. Cool rain on my face.

Do you want more work?

Pause. What should I say?

He continues without my answer.

I need to use a model more often than these classes. His accent makes his English round and lilting, but not with a Hispanic taste. *If you need more work…* Hands me a white card with his right hand. I look down at it whilst he speaks. *I'll pay you the same rate as here.*

His left hand wanders towards the rainy sky. It is not concentrating on where the rest of his body is.

He is expectant.

I don't know. I say, *Oh.* At the same time, I am watching the letters fall softly, like snow, off the business card.

Don't ring too late. Or too early. I can give you directions when you call.

He doesn't say anything else. Watches me. Am I allowed to leave?

My name's Eric.

5

Should I tell him my name? Him and this strange arm, strange accent, frowning at me?

Laura, Soy Laura

He doesn't say anything else. I turn back and walk away. I picture his left hand waving at my back, slowly and sadly, while I walk away in the rain.

When I arrived in the Pais Vasco it was raining. It didn't stop for a week. The dark sky on wet hills outside the city. The rain covered my tracks. It dispersed my scent. Flooded out my mother tongue. I couldn't understand a word that anybody said. When it stopped raining the air was heavy, bulky on my shoulders and my moist clothes. Nothing could dry. The sky every day frowning until it was too dark to make her out. In the streets the stone and brick were dark and saturated. When the sky split open and finally there was the hot and still heat of a sudden and early summer, my curtains still retained their dank smell from the stale water that had been sitting in them for so long with the rains. Some of the stale Spanish, whispered and shouted in the room years before, chipped off in flakes from the walls and window. In my small, cheap room the water had spat through the gash at the top of my broken window and fallen where it had fallen for so long, making a dark, smudgy line on the floorboards. It was a boundary between the rug and the lines of sharp sun that cut the floorboards into window-frame squares.

I lie near the window sometimes, next to the line that the water has made. I am scared because I have left home and I don't know why sometimes. But I know that I don't miss home or the people that I left behind. I like hearing the muffled sounds of the streets and feeling the squares of light that tickle my legs, falling in through the window. Spain has a different light to England. It is clearer. Lighter. There is thick music from next door. I can feel my slack pulse. I feel a little sick. Or hungry? No, sick. I hear laughter. Uncover my stomach. Pull dress up. Feel hip bones. Smooth shell-curve of abdomen. Young, fresh skin. Mine. Someone used to tell me not to touch myself. That I did it too much. That I *thought* about myself too much. But I like it. Someone. I like to lie here whilst I feel a little sick and comfort myself. Eventually it will help me fall asleep.

I arrive for my second session. The man, Eric, is the first student again. I undress in the bathroom but I am not sick again, I didn't eat anything before I arrived this time. I am not as nervous, but I feel light and giddy. When I enter the studio there are more students than the last time. He is still the one who directs me. I can feel him watching as I remove my gown. He is very precise as he directs my poses and none of the other students seem to care; they just put their heads down and concentrate. When I walk through them during the break, they are eager and embarrassed again, just like the last time. They are embarrassed because they have seen me spread-legged-naked. I watch the man as he draws me. As the class progresses, his left arm becomes loose and disengaged from his body. When he concentrates on a particular part of his drawing, the arm could be gently waving at the ground, and when he is looking tired it could be shaking. I am repulsed. I am interested. He is older than most of the other students. His hair is not grey yet. I study him as he studies me, staring at my every part. I see the arm hair that tickles from under his cuffs. His strong, blue eyes. His ugly arm.

I see a drawing of his for the first time during the break. He has left with most of the others to have coffee. I am in front of his easel. The first sketch is a study of my arm, outstretched and tensed. I can see the edges of rough skin on my elbow, the bones of my wrist, delicate, like bird bones, faint hint of muscle in the shoulder and bicep. Stroke my own arm whilst I examine the drawing, feel its loveliness. He has captured it beautifully. I look like I think I should. Beautiful. The young man from the first class returns from his coffee. He tries to talk to me in English again. His sketches are so ugly. I smile and walk away from him. Hide in the bathroom until the break is over.

After the class, Eric is waiting in the doorway of the café again. We look at one another. His gaze pierces me. I feel the blue eyes skewering my words as they fall out of my mouth in chunks.

I am settled in my room now. I have more time.

He does not respond. He stares.

I could ring you this week…if you like.

Still nothing. I think that his accent is Dutch. His blue-eyed, strong-bodied, light-skinned accent. The lilt of his voice reminds me of the Europoort coast in Holland. I went there every summer from when I was ten until I was fifteen with my family. I remember walking on the beach under the sun. A cool sun. It wasn't unlike here, except more remote. You could have run and run on that beach and not seen anybody.

I speak again. The accent of his silence in my head.

You know, for the modelling.

The silent beach. Cool in the sunlight.

I wonder if he has been waiting for me after all. Or if he still even wants me to do it. If he still even wants me. Maybe I have imagined it, and maybe the business card that I hadn't been able to read was in my imagination. Finally he speaks.

Yes. If you have the time.

Dutch accent.

He walks away, in the same direction that I want to take. I wait for him to fade into the weak street lights. When I cannot see him, I follow behind.

I walk. The smiling young man who spoke broken English from the class catches me up. I remember how embarrassed he was in the first class when I flashed my skin at him and watched him stare. He tries to talk to me. I reply, stilted, both of us stumbling over our words. He walks me all the way to my building. In the back of my mind the strange, ugly hand is slowly dragging its fingers across the inside of my skull.

The smiling young man and I don't have very much to say to each other. He is called Marcos, and he hasn't even taken off his shoes, but just shoved his pants down just like he shoved me. I told him to be rough and now he is fucking me against the wall, and if I turn to the side I can look out of my old, broken window. He seemed so smiling and sweet and stumbling in the class but I

8

have teased him so much that now he is sweating and fierce. My legs are parted and he has all of my weight on him, his hands digging into my buttocks whilst he moves, banging my head against the wall. When he moans and speaks it is in Spanish. He doesn't look me in the eye but kisses me quickly and frequently. His foot slips a little and his left finger digs into my thigh as he steadies himself. I think that there will be a bruise there because it hurts, but I don't care. I push him down onto the floor and bite him hard on the shoulder so that he yelps. When he has finished he tries to hold me, but I don't want to be held and I don't put up with it for very long. He tells me that he will see me in the next class, that he lives down that street there and to the left, number 47, *piso B-izquierda*, that maybe we should go out for a drink, *tomar una caña*, he says, his old sweet smile returning. I smile, say *Adiós*.

When I left England it was early in the morning. There were birds singing. Sky was a cold, yawning blue. On the train to the airport there was a drunk opposite me, sleeping and stinking of alcohol. He had wet himself, yawning, turning and dripping down onto the train floor, the smell spreading through the tired old train that had seen it all before. I didn't know what to do so I stared and didn't move away. Just sat in the cloud of stench and watched him. The airport was confusing and I stood watching the departure board for an hour, until an attendant, approaching me for the fourth time, asked me, *Can I call somebody for you miss, are you really okay?* I moved. Went to a desk. The poster of Spain behind the ugly, squat travel agent showed the sun shining and a horse, rearing on its hind legs, with a long white mane. It said: *Visit Spain!* I thought that maybe it was right, that maybe I should visit Spain. The travel agent looked as though she had drawn her face on with make-up; her orange skin and lines of lips and eyebrows. I hoped that I wouldn't look like her, ever. She sold me a one-way ticket for the first plane to Spain. I enjoyed using my credit card because they had threatened that I had no money anyway and would be helpless on my own. She had told me that I needed her and that I couldn't survive on my own.

Well, I had left all by myself, and then I had paid for the plane, and then the first bus out of the airport, and the first week of sleeping in a little hostel. Then I found the room and the modelling job in the café, and my landlady, who is called Inma, like the word 'immaculate', told me that she could help me to learn Spanish. I had never thought about learning a different language but it felt right, it felt as though I was learning to be another person. And I could be anyone that I wanted to.

E ric lives in an apartment. It is on the other side of the river to my little room. As I walk there, the streets become quieter and quieter. No shops any more. No restaurants. More green. Trees playing the sunlight through their leaves and it flickering in my eyes, blinding me one moment and leaving neon dazzle on my shut eyelids the next. Walking up the steep hill with the heat becoming stronger and deeper. Houses and old gates half-open. Gardens with bleached grass. Cats. Old houses. Quiet. The hot, hot air. Clawing at the ground and around my feet. I pant like a dog. The apartment is in a large, old building that sits, haughty, on the crest of the hill. Windows are black eyes, watching me. The grass is yellow, empty, broken lawn. I stand in the porch, quiet but for my breathing. Heat crammed in beside me in the shade, damp on me. Smothering. I pause, my skin soaked, hair flat and warm from the sun.

The pause becomes minutes.

I go up the stairwell.

Knock on the door.

The sound of footsteps. Old wood creaking. Closer. I stand. Do not know what to do. Then there is the crack of the door and he is standing looking at me, all cool and dry. I soak into the doorway and stare wide-eyed at him. He says nothing. I want to hear him say that I am late but he says nothing.

We enter his open apartment. He stands me in the corner of a cleared area next to large windows. There is an easel, a long-necked lamp and a chair at the side of the space. He brings me some water. He tells me to change in the corner. He doesn't leave as I begin to remove my shirt. He just watches me while I undress.

The sunlight shines into the room to form a lit stage in front of the easel. I undress here. Slow. Flick my shirt behind me. Remove my socks. Feel dry, hard floor under each toe. Drop down my pants. The material slides smooth over my legs.

He is still watching me.

The light sliding over naked skin, heating me. His left arm conducts the summer-hot day. He still does not move. Does not speak. I look at him as my pants fall down. His eyes are past mine. They are on me. All over.

I turn. Crouch to push my clothing further away.

Stand up straight.

There is a change. An indrawn breath.

The light in the room clears from yellow to white. Shadows, sleek and growing from the corners. Dark sheets on a sofa, crumpled like frowns.

Air, hot, and creeping slowly around the room.

I look around and turn to face him again.

He is different. His eyes are at my thigh level. Eyes, digging into my skin like Marco's fingers, there, where he left a bruise. The mark blooms under Eric's eyes. Feel it pulsing. Heating up.

Turn around.

I turn.

Bend.

I bend my body forward.

Further. Keep your legs straight.

The muscles up the backs of my legs tight as I bend at the waist.

Move your right leg a little. Apart now.

I obey.

Further.

Feel my bra tilt forward and the wires dig a little into my breasts. My vest slides up my back. Feel my blind skin and spine in the air. Want to move my legs, to bend them. I do not. Hear his steps. Want to turn my head and see him. He sits down. Uncomfortable, weird position. Hear the moving of his hand on paper.

Be still.

Feel all my blood pushing towards my chest and head. Tell myself to relax. To be calm.

But I cannot.

I can see only the floorboards under the increasing, hot white light. Hear the charcoal. Shut my eyes and listen. At first his hand strokes are sweeping and long but then the dusty sound tightens and quickens. His concentration is in the movements of the charcoal on the paper. The sound of the black dust imprinting my image. Heat bounces from the floor onto my feet. It flares in the bottom of my legs.

Open my eyes.

The light from the window spreads further around me. Illuminating. He uses many sheets of paper. Each one makes a dry sound as it is flipped over. The heat burns slow up my legs. My arms out, steadying me. Floating ahead of my body to counteract my weight. My thighs quiver a little. Hands grab and open at the air. Bra digging in. Cheeks heavy with saliva. Hair dropping down over my face.

Think about fucking Marcos. Not seeing his face, just my hair, dangling down and blinding us.

Shiver between my thighs. Body tired from this pose. Let the aches hold me. The shivering and the heating in my legs and cunt become bigger and bigger trembles. Hands contracting and opening. Aching and trying to hold the hot air. The light. I see it between the trying, reaching fingers.

Eric moves. Still no words.

Hear the paper in his hand, rustling as he presses himself upwards from the chair. It warps as he walks.

Comes closer.

Warping very close to me. I am blinkered with hair. Can only stare at the floor, fingers and hair. Have not been told to do anything else. He is close. Feel air on my white, sunless skin. Feel heat. Creeping out of my legs and cunt, all over me. Breaking a sweat out.

Want to move away. I want to move. Move.

He touches me.

Shock. Cold and nauseous. A hot finger.

Strong. He presses the finger into my bruise.

He pushes the side of the bruise that is more turgid and raised than the other. I flinch. The shock has been quick and is filling through my body. He does not speak. His finger waits on my skin as my body shivers.

He presses more.

Sore pain of the blood clot sears under the fingers.

Move away, I think. Move far away.

I do not move.

I snap a look; he has knelt behind me.

Feel his breath on my legs. He presses the bruise harder. He wraps his other fingers around my leg. Fingertips feel dry. His skin is not soft or hard. The fingers press, stronger and stronger. Feel his touch hard on the skin, the soft, down, baby-flesh of my inner thigh.

It hurts the bruise so much. My leg buckles a little with the pressures. Still, he does not say anything. Hear him as he settles down onto the floor.

Removes his hand.

I breathe.

I had forgotten to before.

Move my head round. Very slow.

He does not notice.

Can see my hair. Side of his head and shoulder.

He is on the ground. Face close to my thigh. My bruise.

Keep moving my head, stretch my neck. His concentration is tight on that one spot. He does not care about the rest of me. I hold my gaze. Examine him.

His back is curved round so that his chest is a hollow. Neck pushes head forward to my body. His knees bent, kneeling.

His left hand is a fist. Arm bent slightly at the elbow, fist alongside leg. It relaxes and shuts like a beating heart. Human fist, same size as a human heart. It beats as quick as mine. With each movement, the arm twists and untwists, the shoulder turns and unturns. The fingers squeeze and pulse, relax.

His body breathes with the beat of his left hand. His mouth open. Tongue lying in the saliva dark pool of his bottom jaw. It glistens and works itself into his gums. Eyes wet and shiny and white.

He is alive and pulsing with a visible beat. A hot, fast blood. Our breath the same. Our sweat acrid, a stench in the bright, bright light. Blotting out all but what it illuminates on this stage.

Beside his right leg are several sheets of paper. Crumpled at the corners, the sheets are blank.

His right arm is raised.

It is raised and hesitating before my thigh. The fingers are outstretched. They mirror my fingers that reach out in front of me, grasping for balance.

They are tense, shaking slightly. The shaking of a wrong chord with the beating hand-heart of his left fist. All out of balance. His fingers are ready and reaching for my leg.

Our breath stops being the same. I stop it with one gulp of air and then I forget to breathe again.

Blink. I turn my head to stare at hair and my fingers and white, hot floor. Blink again and stay in the darkness of eyelids.

The same moment his fingers grasp me, stronger than before. Press and don't let go of my pain, my searing bruise. At the same moment, his breath bursts out of him in a hiss. A sound of high-pitched piano-key chord rings from my nerves and cunt and escapes from my mouth, hitting my fingers and the floorboards in a spitty, hot escape.

So Inma rented out another room at the end of the hallway, which I hadn't seen before because the door had always been shut. It is like my room, plain. Small. I looked through the door as she aired it and I looked through when the new boarder arrived. Bedraggled in the heat, she has very fine, snappable wrists and ankles and deeply tanned skin with white eyes digging deep under a brow of dark hair. Inma fusses her because she is thin and silent and begins to cook for us most nights. Sit around the table, my Spanish words pick around the food. New girl says nothing, Inma pecking at her, staccato. *Amorcito, debes que comer. No te gusta la comida? Quieres que te prepare algo diferente? Debe que ser diferente la comida Argentina, no?* I clean the plates. New girl doesn't help to clean up. She is a legato-slur, smoothly gone into her room.

She leaves throughout the day, but not at regular times. She leaves her door ajar and I can see through the gap at the hinges. She moves, sits. Soundless.

Dresses,

Sometimes she is gone all day, and sometimes she doesn't come out of her room at all and is silent behind the closed door.

Undresses.

She does not give me anything.

Her name is Bea.

I t was raining.

I was about to enter the building when Inma overtook me and held the door, smiling. *Hola, mi niña.*

I smiled back widely at her words. Sounds.

We almost walked past Bea, crouching in the hall. Her form in the corner of my eye could have been an umbrella, splayed and sopping, leaning against the wall.

Bea, Bea! Qué pasó?

Inma bent down to her, touching the head and face, making it turn towards her. White eyes looked up, expressionless. Waking Bea from a dream. I thought about the name, Bea. Be.

Bea!

Inma's hands quickened around her and tried to get her to stand. Slowly Bea stood and said, staring into Inma's face,

Nada.

Water flowing off her, dribbling down the little tinkling fingers.

Estoy bien.

Inma pushed her up the stairs, her shivers shaking through us, and pushed her into her room.

When Inma came out of Bea's room, I slipped behind her into the kitchen. She slammed the fridge door. Put some milk on to boil.

15

Her deft, quick hands. The lid of the milk, pour thick, opaque stream, pan, pan handle, metal, click of lighting, flame blue.

She disappeared again into the hallway.

There was the sound of a heavy thing smacking down from the window in the kitchen. The window looked out into the tall atrium in the centre of four blocks of flats where washing lines were cringing under the heat of the corrugated plastic roof.

The milk formed a skin, creasing into itself as the bubbles formed slow then fast.

You could look up and down the atrium, hear people, see them through the angles of their windows. Hear people dropping things, shouting, sometimes talking very quietly.

Milk expanding in the pan.

I opened the window. A sheet had fallen, spread out and wet, onto the ground floor.

Inma talking. Loud. quick.

The sheet would need to be returned to its owner. Re-washed. Hung out again to dry.

Louder back into the kitchen.

She scowled at the milk, crispy dry on top of the cooker. Quick wet cloth. Wiping the smell away. She didn't understand Bea. Muttering.

She pushed the milk and cocoa at me, watching me for a moment. I mixed it whilst she reached up, crinkled arm-skin extending, and took down a bottle from which she drank, as always with ice, from the same cut glass tumbler that waited for her on the window ledge.

Picked up the cocoa in front of me and handed it back to me. She was angry and more like a mother now.

Es para ella, la Bea.

More and more like a mother.

Pushed me out, motioning towards the room whilst drinking from her glass.

I did not knock. She was lying in her bed. Long, wet hair. The sopping clothes were not there, towels draped around her.

Bea.

The brows stretched up towards me as I am saying her name.

16

Clean skin. Dry cotton t-shirt.
  She reached out and took the cup.
  Gracias, Lauw-ra.
  She turned away.

I let myself out.

I magining, itching, the hungry biting of teeth all over. Rain
   falls on the hills, the city, on everything. Excess water drips
   down over my body, imaginary milk, falling with the rains,
rich and heavy outside the windows and pooling through the
cracks in the sills and window glass. Feeling is constant and ripe,
as though it has been there for a long time, yet at the same time,
is fleeting and could leave at any moment. The hot air moves
between the sky and the rain, makes me sweat. Standing, watching
from my window the water, spitting from roofs. Rebounding and
spraying down. Sweat blooms and falls down my sides. Watching,
waiting. White clear sweat it is. It sours like milk, smells a slow,
rank odour. Rain is heavy, strong. Waiting, waiting. The heat of
the summer becoming unbearable. Peaking. Downpour like the
strange Spanish language, both everywhere. I don't understand
either. Have to accept them both. Posing at the window. Wanted
to be further under the rain, not teased by it here in the window.
Sit down like a dog. I know that it would wash away the sweat.
Would wash. Would wash. Think about dirty skin and the hair
on my body. Rain spits. Rain spits. I miss. Is he underneath the
rain? His clothes would be wet. Sit down with legs spread like a
dog. From the window, I can see the hills. They are soaking and
blooming open, drinking and drinking this wet meal. In the dryer
days of the summer I walked in those hills and felt the needles
of the flies there, eating everywhere on my body. What would the
flies do now, now that the raindrops were the size of eggs, hitting
the sky, the trees, the hills? Standing, soaking, watching. Rain spits.
Breasts feel as though they will bruise and split open like fruit.
Overwhelming, it is. There is no sound inside the apartment but
the rain, falling, waiting and waiting, itching.

It is early evening. Bea's door is shut. Pouring rain. The last time that I saw him, he was still sitting on the floor, still looking at where my bruise had been. Did not say goodbye. Session over. Eyes all vacant and quiet. Sopping, falling rain. Soon I am working in the café again. I think that I will see him there, that he might want to see me again. I want to wash myself, fall with the wet, wet, falling water…

…the water is falling around me. Not in the street, but inside, from above, the wall, the ceiling. Move away and watch for a moment. Watch the leaking roof become a flood. Move sopping book, plate, rug, all away. Almost fall over Inma as I run and turn into the kitchen.

Eh, eh! Que pasa?

Inma's arms up in surprise, her bright face alight. She is looking down at me, even though she is as short as a child. I speak at her fast.

Pause. No movement, no reaction. Nothing. I lead her back, touch her arm, curve my hand around it and take her there. Her warm, little arm in my hand. Limp, she follows me and when we get there the sound of water is around us.

Pause. No movement. Pause, then she goes, Inma.

She rushes to the telephone. Leaves me staring at the water, everywhere. It is calm and fast. A cold breeze comes off it, like sweat rising. Inma in the kitchen. Under the sink, gets a bucket. Returns, puts it under the stream and it comes up, water hitting her hands. Dirty water.

Watch it. Inma comes back and stands next to me. *Ahora, ahora, hablo con el hombre. Llega muy rápido. Esta en un otro piso. Hay el mismo problema.*

Tongue my letters. *Es un edificio muy viejo.* Test out words. Inma doesn't reply; they don't work.

18

We watch the bucket fill up. Watch as Inma wipes water from her face, her damp skin. Old hands. I have felt their soft, dark, damp pulse.

The door sounds and she goes to it. I don't move. Watch the plaster begin to break. It falls in pieces onto the floor, chips and lumps. The voice in the hallway with Inma speaks thick fast. She makes gestures with her hands. He walks into the room; I hear their sounds behind me. Don't say anything. Inma gasps at the sopping plaster all fallen in chunks. The man goes to use the phone and tells Inma to find another bucket. *Vamos!* Feed off each other's excitement. See myself in a reflection again, the water shimmering and making it distort. Their words fast, fluttering around them like birds, skin shiny with excitement and rain.

Back away. Hear the man on the phone. Slowly, slowly, he is almost shouting.

Si, si! Hay un grand problema, si si! Todo el cuarto!

My back against the front door. Turn around and away. Go.

Instantly wet. No need to find a doorway to shelter in; it has overcome me already. Accept it. Drenched. Walk.

Walk. Sound of rain.

Hitting me.

No people on the streets anymore. Not even the dogs.

Walk. The rain sound deafening.

Up the hill. Breath quick quick.

Light changing in the sky behind the rain. The water blackening under the bridge.

Calm and cool in my head. Damp. A cool breeze coming off the water, off me. Walk through the gate, the path, the porch. Quick up the stairs. Dry, closed space of the stair shaft. Steps again, listen to my steps, the only sound. Louder and louder in a beat.

Open the door to his apartment. Stand on the threshold.

Sudden.

Silence.

Except for

19

the muffled beat of the rain.

Of the dryness. Beat of my feet becomes my heart.

Wake up. Go.

Stop.

Open, dry room and the long-necked lamp, standing with its bowed head in front of me as though sleeping. Not needed now.

Pulse, beating hard and heavy.

To my side…

The man stands beside the sofa. His shirt is half on. He has stopped in surprise at the sight of me, dripping and standing still in his doorway.

I blink. Blink. I stare.

His chest is naked. Sandstone skin. Naked. Bare. Moving.

Pulse.

I stare.

I see him.

His muscles are defined across his chest. On the right side they are smaller. There are four clean, pink scar lines there. They are raised and bright. They cross over one another and all but one of them start around his waist, in the soft curve of skin. The other one begins on the collar bone and gracefully leans down over the right breast. Leading in curves, they finish at different points of the chest and plough clean, hairless paths above the belly button, apart from the lowest. This carves the longest line, right across the gut.

Body hair is dark with a sheen of grey. It grows in patches around the scar lines. He is tall; my head would be level with his shoulder if we were to stand together.

The left shoulder has a rough and heavy purple clot. This scar is the most prominent. There is a wide, neat circle of hairless skin dipping in from around its edge. The skin puckers and stands up in places so that a landscape is made. It is a crater. In the centre is a raised knot of purple, stretched skin.

The gradients of two other circular wounds are varied in the same manner. They peak where the skin ties into itself. The skin then collapses around these knots, pushing them further upwards. These two circles have the same red shade of the blood that is sitting under the skin. They are similar sizes. One imitates a nipple, between the real, right-hand nipple and the crease of the armpit. It is closely missed by the second highest line-scar. The other aims for the belly button, but higher and on the left side. The hair creeps closer, in two cleanish circles, around these scars. The hair is not as scarce as around the large, purple clot. It closes in more.

The real nipples are small and brown, with raised pores scattered around them. The forearm hair has less grey. It is thick and barely broken. The hands are worn and have many small scars. I have never noticed those scars before, all over his hands. Why have I never noticed them? Some are visible from only very close. If he were to spread the fingers of his working, right hand, they would intimidate the span of my open fingers. The pads of the finger-skins are thick. These right-hand fingers have deft, tuned muscles. They stretch beautifully up through the forearm. I can see them, tensing. The left hand has muscles that are tight and thin. They can quiver. They are violin strings. The skin through this arm is slightly paler than the right. Weak blood flow. There are no outstanding scars on this left arm, just the purple clot on the shoulder. It looks like a pin through a doll's arm-joint.

I stare and see everything. Stare at the skin, the hair. The dark, purple mark across the shoulder. Hideous. See dirt and scars. Dark, dark skin and hair. Like an animal.

My staring and sudden presence, sudden staring trance. He recovers from the initial surprise. Blink as he pulls the shirt up.

Covers himself.

I still stare. Water drips from my hair into my eyes. Drops make a tapping sound on the wooden floor below me. Clear, tap-tap-tap. Blink my eyes. They are burnt dry. Can still see the scars lain out on my eyelids like a map of stars.

Qué?

Words rap out of his mouth.

Qué quieres?

More silence and drip-drip.

He repeats in English.

What do you want? You are here.

Look up and then down at my feet and the cold puddle around me.

21

I… Don't know where to look. *Lo siento…* Back away slightly. Glance at the lamp. Its sleeping head turned slightly towards me. I have interrupted its slumber.

He *Speak English* interrupts me.

I am so sorry, I….I just. My wall, the water. Falling rain, out like words. But quickly stops again.

Stare and stand at each other in the dry, lit room with the silence.

He can fasten a shirt with one hand very quickly. Very deftly.

I start again. Spatter of rain. *I'm sorry. It's just that, my wall has fallen in and I had to get out.*

His left arm sudden, waving upwards toward me quickly. He ignores the movement. Expectant. Holding his top button with his right hand. My own arms still flapping, uncontrolled and trying to explain.

I had to leave because a man arrived, to, you know, fix it. And. And…

His eyes examine up and then down me slowly. There is no more surprise in his arms or his eyes. He is calm and closed in. Concentrates on me

And I just started walking and – *I'm sorry, I didn't think. I just ended up here.* Twist my foot, to leave. Do not twist my body. There is that map again. It is scarred stars. It is neon over my eyes and I stare still, intruding and contaminating with my wet clothes, my wet mist. Clothes grip and knickers, cold. Cold breasts. Cold lips and cheeks. Stare at him still.

He does not say anything.

He is not polite. Does not offer me anything. Shiver. Standing. The lamp does not move in its sleep.

Walks in front of me and towards the kitchen. Stands looking back towards his bed with his hand on the side of the hob. He looks back towards the sofa where he was standing before. Except there is no exposed body there now. With beautiful marks, written on his skin.

I will still see you tomorrow. In the class.

He instructs.

Thick heartbeat. *Yes. Um, yes, of course.*

And his back turns. Suddenly. His arm supports his body

slouching towards the sink on the back wall, left arm out and conducting gently, the sound of the rain. Head down.

I stand moments longer. But he does not move anymore.

I blink and drip. Breathe in. Feel for the door behind me. Step out and down the lonely stairs. Walk back into the rain. Out of the garden to the sopping road. The sopping world, running at my feet. The new map of stars, scars, dazzling and blinding me to the cold.

About to ring my own bell when Inma walks out. Wants to know what I am doing in the rain. Why had I forgotten my key? Why I am so wet? Pointless questions; the rain is still strong. And why am I standing around down here – she has no time to make me cocoa. Tells me that there are two men in my room, fixing and plastering. She is staying with her sister. I should sleep in her room. She is back tomorrow. *Que todo bien mañana*. Make some cocoa and change clothes. Be dry. She grasps my arms and stares into me. No sound but the water. Strong grip. Flicks open her umbrella then walks away down the street. I wait. I go and find my keys. I do not change and I do not make a cocoa. I walk down the black street. And it is still raining. There are still stars.

Marcos is as wet as I am very quickly. I am wet all over. He has come down the stairs and outside to meet me. I crouch in the hallway. I am like Bea was in my stairwell. I do not want to go into his apartment. He lives with his family. He is a child. I don't want to meet them and be in their dry flat. But I want to bring him back to mine and soak him on the way. We do not speak much. Sound of our steps, keys in the door. He reaches his hand to touch my waist as we ascend the stairs. Tries to kiss me while I open the flat door. Go to tiptoe past my room, but the door is shut anyway. There is a radio on in there. Damp, damp everything. Have hold of his arm. Make him leave the light on. Watch him while he waits because I make him wait and watch. Don't let him take my clothes off. I do it myself, slowly. I like the mirror on Inma's wardrobe doors. He digs his clothes off quick. I like her remnants; crucifix, a hairbrush filled with hair. I look at them whilst he is on top of me, digging away. He looks at my face and down my body, back to my face, staring at where my eyes are. There is a flicker of a person passing the doorway. I know that it is Bea. It passes the crack in the hinge. After a few moments it passes again as he groans. I barely move. Speaks while he moves and sweats and comes. His naked chest is hairless and paler than I thought it would be. Thin and smooth. Clean. He smells of his home and food.

Discard him. He moans and tries to leach himself around me in the bed. Radio. Flickering and pad of little footsteps pacing. I get up and put some clothes on, tell him I'm going to *el baño*. When I open the door she is not there. When I return I flick him away and out of the door, past the oblivious work men and out, like a droplet of rain from my back. He tries to look me in the eye and touch my waist again at the apartment door. Out.

Finally he is shut out quietly behind me. Slide, slowly, down the door and sit with my ass-bones pushed into the bottom of it. Breathe. The damp pants and top that I dragged on quick to cover me smell of sex and sweat. Stars are in front of my eyes again.

When I stand up, the blood rushes through me and I cannot see for a few moments. Then the apartment and the noise, radio and faint rain, comes back into view. Walk back towards Inma's room. Pass by Bea's. she is in there.

I know that she is in there.

I ready my eyes to stare through the gap of her door hinge so that I can see her, like she saw me before. I look. I make a photo of her with my eyes, and whip round, I am back towards Inma's room. The corner of the bottom of Bea's bed is very close to the hinge of the door. Before I arrived at that hinge-gap of light through the door, she had stopped what she was doing with her hands, half lying, looking
down.

She is on her bed, looking down at herself, with her legs spread open and half bent.

Her body is very snappable. Long lines. Hardly any body hair.

24

Her nipples are dark. Her sides smooth lines. Long fingers. They reach and hold open her cunt and that is where she is looking.

I make a photo with my eyes.

Her pubic hair is fine and it barely grows as far as the creases of her thighs. It is almost the same colour as her tan skin. In between the hair her cunt is not pink and sleek. Instead, she has a pattern, almost inside her, of red-purple and yellow circles inside one another, deep and buried and breaking up her pinky skin. There are many circles, many swollen marks. They are winking with moisture. With pus.

I make a photo very quick.

Snap.

Look in her eyes is fierce and quick. Like catching an animal eating a carcass.

A stretched, red feeling inside my chest. It expands tight and spreads up and through my throat, while I look down, blinking, and see stars and circles behind my eyelids. I sit on the hallway floor, beside the door.

I close my eyes completely. Too much for me. They are dazzled. The rain still has not stopped.

For a moment more, there is silence. So much silence today. So many bodies and so much sweat. I hear her call out.

She calls me to her.

Remember the scarred map of stars.

I go.

Place your wrists together.
He speaks while taking hold of my left wrist and pulling it in front of me. I put my wrists together. Palms facing inwards. He lets go of me. Takes a long white cord in his right hand. Left hand is waving at his side. He is tall in front of me. A tall shadow. Can barely make out his white teeth, can see clearly his white eyes. Today, the room is see-through layers of summer light and shades of shadow. His shadow is solid. Black. Blocking

my vision. He lays the cord over my white wrist flesh and pulls one side so that the end of the cord is a few inches below my hands. He takes this end between his index and middle fingers and hooks it around the other side of the cord which hangs heavy off my wrist and coils on the ground. Deft. He takes the hooked cord with his thumb. The material makes a soft sound as it moves against flesh. Thumb pushes it round the hanging side, as though to hook it again, but then the index and middle take it again and feed it up inside the loop around the wrists. Thumb helps. Tightens the cord by pinching one side between index and middle and the other side between fourth and thumb. It is taut. He secures the knot by making another loop. Yanks it all. My wrists wobble towards him, fingers loose and open. He slides the cord through his hand until there is roughly three feet of slack and then he kneels down and places the cord very close to the floor. Its tension pulls my wrists down and makes a curve in my back. Straining against the taut cord. He looks up at me. His eyes are torches. They light up what he sees, what he concentrates on. He blinds me as he stares up into my eyes.

Lift up your foot.

I lift.

I blink at the shadows that appear in my eyes as he moves his eyes downwards and concentrates on tying me up. He loops the cord under and around so that it is tight on my ankle. My balance is unstable. Waver. He ignores this, carries on and ties an identical knot to the one on my wrists. The soft skin on my ankle bones is sensitive as he brushes it. Can feel his breath on me, gentle, but there.

Put your foot down.

It is harder for him to bring the end of the cord through the knot this time because there is a lot more slack. He drops the cord onto the floor and takes it up again from near the knot, pulling it. He does this twice and he has the end. He stands. His eyes shine down into mine. One moment. Heat of summer has seeped into the room. It sticks in the patches of light. It sticks in the light I feel from his eyes. I am shorter now, my strained back and low wrists held by the cord. Have to twist my neck to look up at him. He drops the end of the cord through the vertical rod of the window pane where the handle is. Ties the same knot. Yanks it, shining and tight.

He takes the cord attaching my wrists and ankle. His hand makes a fist around the cord. He pushes this fist towards my stomach. His knuckle comes closer towards me, level with the boneless space above belly button and below rib-cage. Very close. Can smell faint smell of lived-in skin, its sweet smell, fresh sweat. Knuckles touch and press into me. I back up. It is hunched and awkward to move. Cord is made taut between ankle and window pane. My weight pulling against it makes the window open. His fist stops pushing. I stop moving. The fist retracts. The light becomes brighter. He is backing up, is at his seat. His shadow is darker in this light. Sun begins to pool around my feet and I am almost in the centre of the modelling space with the pane open at its fullest. He takes up his large drawing pad and fingers through his tin of charcoals with his right hand. The left hand calm, resting by his side.

Move towards the floor.

Taut. I move. Stomach muscles tingle-tense. Press my body down. I bend my knees. Try to keep balanced. I am squatting, wobbling. Looking at him.

He glares.

No. Go onto your knees. Spread them. Put your thighs on the floor.

Drop my knees forward from the squat onto the floor. Twist my feet out from underneath my buttocks and to the sides. Floor lukewarm with sunlight. Silent. His fingers shove the charcoal against paper. Breathe. I curve deeper into position. Calf and thigh spread out more onto the floor. Eventually, cunt touches briefly the shiver of the floorboards. Wince. He does not respond. Push it down to touch again and the shiver stays a little longer. Tickles me more and more, up inside my body until it is against the back of my spine. There is pain growing there, through my backbone. It is tight and pulled tighter with the tension made by my bound wrists.

He still does not respond to me. Sound of the charcoals and leaves of paper moving. The sheets are illuminated by him. Eyes flicker between paper and my body. His black shape is darker and darker as the light in the room changes in my eyes. There is summer and his concentration and his shadow. The shades and sizes warp. Space between us is unclear. Uncomfortable. I am heating up with the summer and his eyes. Moist under my arms and in the line where my thighs touch. My spine heats with more and more pain. Dull thud begins to sound in my ankle under the cord. Summer outside is silent. Try to gulp. Mouth and throat are dry and rough. Blinking is heavy. He does not notice these things. There is only the sound of the charcoals and the leaves of paper moving.

I want to see your neck.

He stands. Slack thud of the drawing pad dropping onto the floor. His dry shadow, solid and smooth, begins to lap up the oil-slick puddles of sunshine that are around my feet. From my view his broad shoulders block out light, white and blind, from the window. As he comes closer, my eyes are level to his thighs, dry with dusty marks of charcoal scratched over cotton trousers. His torch-eyes find me under the shadow that is now as deep as the base of my painful spine and creeping, like a tide, up each nub of bone. His crouching hand pulls smooth over my head, pulling hair together. He pinches it. Can feel his middle fingers working it through an elastic band. Hurts. I look up. Can see vaguely through the shadow where his exposed collar bones meet in a deep hollow of throat. Peaks of scar tissue planted with body hair. Skin smell again, sweat smell becoming sour. His bright eyes squint my sight as the tide of his shadow covers me more and more, cool and silent. Crack my neck back to face up to him. I am staring into his headlight eyes. My hair very tight. Feels as though it holds my head in position.

His finger reaches around my neck.

It presses the straining, fragile bone at the base of my skull. His fingertip skin is thick. I feel it make an imprint. The pressure twists slightly on contact and his blinding gaze twists with it. The skin stretches with the movement and pain is spreading across my back and deep into my thighs. He presses harder. Shakes through my chest with that same heavy feeling. A final press brings me, for one moment, closer to the charcoal on the cotton trousers. He blinks and all is dark. My body submerged by that shadow. He brands a mark on me with that finger. Deep, blood-rich and pulsing mark.

His step backwards is near silent. By his left side his hand is quivering. Sunlight inches back into the room. It uncovers the deep, creeping shadow.

The shadow laps away.

There is a deep, deep, powdery breath. He sits. There is summer again.

Inhale.

Inhale more and more.

As much as you can.

I pull hard against the cord as I suck in air. There is no give.

The summer light that is around and in between us flickers. Floating and calm, the dust that is in the air blinks on and off with it. Lines of stronger light cut through the weaker light, then everything goes black. Then light again. Summer returns with each flicker. It is hot. The sections of sunlight and daytime in the room fill the spaces between him, the cord, me. It shuts off, with each flick, the creeping, increasing sound of sex in me. Gone. Instead there is cold clammy between my legs and in the dark space of my armpits. There is the twist of threads in the muscles of his arms as they push and smear the charcoals. His hand makes marks against the paper, quick and free, all curves and flecks. The cord allows me a similar curve of movement. The curve of me failing to get away. Tension brings out lines and specific marks on my body that were not there before. Cold sweat flushes through my forehead and back. I pull, and panic is there, pulling with me and trying to get away from the window pane. All that sickly light puking in from the window. It is pushing me in, further to this room, further into the summer that has already infested the room from outside with heat. Sweat. White eye contact with him. He holds it steadfast. His hand is free and blind on the paper. Summer is looped around both wrists and an ankle, extending out my spine as it reaches to stay close to the window pane and yet pushes to get away. Thrusting curve, going behind and stretching through my back. But stay close. That cord is cutting more and the window pane is not breaking. But get away.

Get away.

That tide of shadow has washed away.

The white light that is left is blinding me.

He leans forward. I look to him. Continues to draw whilst I pull more. I can't stop this pulling and thudding through me. Tighter and tighter grip on wrists. My heart pulls with me against the window pane. The white sunlight oozes around my toes and thickly spreads the sweat further up into me. I begin to slide with the sweat on my feet. He sees right through it all and continues to draw it as though there is nothing there. His drawing getting faster and faster, leaves of paper floating lightly around him as he creates and creates. Pull and pull, creeping summer all around. It basks in the fanning air I make with the window pane. The pane flaps and flaps with me as I pull, trying to get out of the cord, cutting my wrist red skin, deeper and deeper with each tug. Smearing feet, brighter light. His body is all that is left of the shadow, in the light of the sweat summer. He is a dark, solid block amongst the air and light and his eyes, white ice shining from this darkness, and deft movement of his hand. Blinding and drowning, and the cord will not break.

Mouth is a sodden deep hole that echoes, swallowing each sound that beats loudly inside to get out. I open it and the lips feel gritty as they pull up over the teeth. There is no sound. There is a solid tug and this time I slip, smack onto my knees. The jolt does not budge the cord or the window. It cracks the summer off for several moments before it comes back, and I feel thick slab of tongue between my teeth, mingled with the grit and slop of saliva. It still cannot make any sound. The arc that was in the spine has been overcome by my falling. The muscles are bright, burning, and they cannot move as freely as before. Sore. Knees banged, beating.

He sighs. Stops. The loud smack of the sketchbook cutting through the sunshine. Banging against the wooden floor. He stands up. Shadow shifts. With it, a piece of the sunshine is tilted out of the window. He is coming closer. Nauseating calm as more and more air moves for his shadow and body to approach. The heat making way. There is a smell coming nearer, of sweat. Heavy. His movement is supple, strong and fast towards me. The left arm

30

shakes, right through to the fingers. His right hand moves towards
the knot to free it. Rising taste of bile in my throat mixing with
breath and air. His torch-bright eyes not on me anymore but only
on the knot.

Breath.

Deep, deep breaths.

My damp skin brushing against him a lot with the movement. I
watch our bodies as we touch. My arm with his arm. Naked feeling
of the cloth of his shirt. It is leaving an invisible line of fabric,
stained with scent, along my left arm. I see the little scars on his
hands. They are bright and outstanding and moving as his hand
moves with the cord.

The torch-eyes are turning to me, blinding. They guide my eyes
upwards into his. They penetrate deep as he is tightening the
cord, forcing my wrists into the metal of the window. My wrists
smear into the window. Good yank, shaking all through me. I
cannot move much more. Feeling metal, cord, pulse against cord,
sweat, summer. My blood is louder than the heat now, thudding
through wrists, body and in my ears. His sun-eyes move down and
glare into the broken tension of my body, studying each line. He
stares for several moments. He takes his time. His hand moves
downwards from the knot and covers both of my hands. His
is hot and damp. The fingers wrap and dig around mine slowly.
Feeling bile again, up in my throat. The fingers tighten. Thudding
in my ears, beating so fast that it is almost a constant sound.
Overpowering smell of his sweat. Tighten more. Dig so that I can
feel the bones in my knuckles pressing together. His eyes returning
to mine. I am blinded. Constant pulse. White light. He gives a final
clench, with words spoken soft.

Stop moving.

Out in the sun, can barely see for the white light. Stumble
from the porch and along the path. Feet trip between the
grass and the concrete. Touch the gate, pinch it between
thumb and finger, push it, open it. Out. Close it. Creaking. Shake.

Shaking gently, through whole body. I drop my envelope. It slips open and money sprinkles out on the tarmac. Crouch. Pick it up. Tip forward onto knees, kneel. Suck in some air. Sit for a while.

The white light clouds over with black.

Suck in some air. Sit for a while.

Slow dots of white light and real life come back through into my eyes. Almost a minute, still sitting, waiting for sight to completely return. He has no window that looks onto the street, but turn my head, stare back in the direction of the building. It slides slowly into full view like a slide in a projector. Stones of tarmac stick into my legs. Old woman is nudging slowly along from the other side of the pavement. She asks if I am okay. The stones drop off and new ones stick as my legs scrape around beneath me on the floor. Old-lady wrinkles droop around her mouth and eyes. She has approached me, is standing very close. Hunched. Her hand reaches towards me. At the same time, it shakes. Stare at it and do not move. Woman claws my shoulder. *Qué pasó? Estas bien, cariño?*

I'm fine. I am fine, really.

Woman moves back slightly. Don't bother to even try in Spanish. I reach. Take hold of the hand and stand. Wobble. Old lady puts her arms up towards my shoulder, she can barely reach. Stares at me. Bien? Mejor? I try. Make a half smile. Feel it weak and pale at the edges. I go to crouch again to pick up all the money. Woman has one last stare and turns. Walks on, away. Slowly. She looks back. Ignore her. Stare at the tarmac where the money had been. Blink. Wheeze in more air. Shake more. Eyes cloud with black again, with small dots of light. Sit down again. Put palms down to make me steady. Tarmac stones stick neatly into them.

He instructed me to return ten days later. He is going away with a job. Stand up. Look around in all directions. There is nobody. I don't know what his job is. Begin to walk down the hill. Did not even know that he had a job. Walk as slow as the old woman. The steep hill is nauseous. People are beginning to appear. Some of them half-closed, siesta eyes. They walk past me in the streets. Some look at me, some don't. I pass shops. The luscious park with children playing in the playground. All normal. A Chinese clothes shop. Several Basque restaurants with traditional lettering curving

32

out the names above the doorways. Black letters with yellow backgrounds. Always the same lettering, always *jatetxea*. A small roundabout.

The enormous, calm building that was once a tobacco factory. It sits back from the road behind an open space and some plants, trees, grass. There is tarmac with a striped, raised lump in it and some of the windows in the building are broken. They are the windows to the sides, less obvious. Sharp teeth are left of frosted glass. Main doorway massive, a toothless mouth – black, open, gaping. There is an art exhibition being held there. Bright people stand around the mouth. Slack security guard. Big, bright poster draped on the side of the building. Sweat rings on armpits of chic outfits. Noise. Smells. I blink at it all from the railings. Begin to watch the floor as I move away. There are the solid paving slabs. The curb. The tarmac of the bicycle path. More stripes on tarmac. Try to close my eyes while I carry on towards home. He said not to be late. The regular time, just like the other sessions. Always during the heat of the day, when *todo el mundo* is sleeping inside the shadows of their rooms. I reach the river. Smell of the ocean and fish. Smell of summer. I try to speed up but legs are loose and powerless. Sound of cars, people talking. Lots of people as I cross the bridge – tourists walking slowly and loudly. The smell and sight of the city, the bridge, the day, the water. Put hands up on ears. Look down. Wobble forward, panting and spit sitting inside my throat, until I reach the flat. His flat would be empty and dead without him. Now, the calm dark of the hallway. No people. No noise except my breathing. Heavy. Sweat armpit rings, sweat rolling down my face and body. Spend a lot of time breathing and waiting in this dark where eyes and ears and skin can be calm.

Watching you wash yourself. Bea. Half-light of late afternoon highlights the dirty tub. Grey scum-chipped edges. Your water is dirty. Your skin is dirty. Foot drips onto the damp mat, dangling over. Open thighs lapping the water. I like to imagine that you don't know that I'm here, watching. The open door, mirror in the hallway. Your hands wash and slowly scratch. Noise of water moving around your body, up your belly, licking over each grey rib that is a water mark. Hair chunking from behind ears to over face, lapping your lips. Begin to examine the under-skin of your arms, twisting it red, round. You examine your hands, then your tits, stroking and reacting and rubbing your waist, the deep belly button. Your tanned and dirty skin is different to mine. The shade of your nipples, the sunless skin in your arm-pits.

Between your legs there is that hair the same colour as your skin, like the down of the underbelly of a bird. I can imagine it, but now I cannot see it, or see your hands. It is all under the level of the tub's rim. Imagine I am standing there, dipping my blind hands into the opaque water.

The deep squeak of your foot, bringing it into the water. You stand up. In the bathroom mirror you spread your feet slowly apart, stare yourself. The white, yellow lips of the ulcers have begun to nestle at the very tops of your thighs. Dampened, they are enlarged. Your virus has spread far. Around them the swollen skin looks round and firm. Brown-red. There is less hair covering the two lobes that hang to cover vagina. This makes them look redder, exposed. For the mirror, you open them up and show the smaller lobes, perforated. Long, smoothed lines of swollen skin. As you finger the different places you frown. Wide, low eyes, index finger pushed into a large sore and hiss with pain. Index and middle finger disappear, inside you, up. Move your hand, controlling. Remove them, moist and grey. Face unchanged. Wet hair on the pubis curling and stroking softly at the open sores. A sensual scratch. Sausage strips of sick, swollen skin, pliable and plump between the fingers.

You squat, take shower head, uncurling it from tap. Writhes around as you bring it to your lips, tasting the water, pushing and showing your teeth to it, you drink, thirsty. Kiss it against breast, water seething out from between your skin where it can. You put it to your legs, sores. Your head pushes back a little, as though with pleasure. I want to touch where the water hits you. Want to touch myself. I smell urine – diluted. The water from the shower-head must be diluting it. Your teeth grit, strained eyes, dragging up your cheek bones. You hold it against your cunt for a long time before turning the water off, taking out the plug and lying back, breathing

34

into the bath and the piss that will be mixing with the grey scum in the water all around you.

Your face turns slowly and you open your eyes at me, slowly parting your wet lips. Quickly take my hand up from my pants.

Ven aquí .

You tell me to come to you. I come. I kneel next to the tub. Swish of water and weak urine. Your hand reaches over the edge and your eyes are blinking wide at me. I wince. Hiss of a gasp. Your fingers have curled around my perfect circle of wrist bruises. They are fully in bloom, three days old. Your eyes break from mine. You lift my wrist and search for what made me gasp. I try to get your eyes back into mine but yours are turning around my hand. You reach for the other one. You stare at them, both identical. I stare too. In between them I see through to the tight, goose-flesh skin of your chest. Dripping. You have my eyes in yours again. Your hands are gentle on each of my wrists. You rub slowly each one with your thumbs. Press where my pulse is, where the rope was. We stare and stare. Your lips part slightly. Head tilts slowly to the side. We stare and there is not even the sound of the water moving. Your lips part more and they curve shy up your face. I copy. The rubs of your thumbs become bigger circles and when they pass over the bruise I don't wince again. You pull my hands and arms over the tub. Makes my tits press against the cold edge. My elbows bend and rest on the bathtub lip. Your wash my hands, forearms. My circles. In your water. Soap. Sponge. Your almond-shaped fingertips. Wash me. With my face closer to yours I see the slick locks of hair, fat with water. Wet eyelashes. Whites of your eyes with thin veins only near the corners. Smile is there still. You close it into a circle. Take your hand out of the water. It drips on the base of my skull and pulls it in. Kiss my eye sockets. One by one. Warm lips on the thin skin of eyelid. Then down. Our lips make circles together. Tastes of urine and girl.

Wake up. Blink. Squint. Pieces of your hair are deep nestled in my mouth. The rest of your hair covers my face. Pull them out. Move away from you. You are still

sleeping. Warm, drowsy air escapes a little from the sheets. Your
body, hot and dry. Moving with your breath. Sound of air, slow in
your throat and mouth. Hair smells of grease and you. Touch the
slack curve of your waist. Nothing. I am sticky under my arms,
sweet and comfortable sweat. The light is soft; curtains are drawn.
Sheets are dirty. Their smell is strong of you and sleeping. Room
is bare. Dry, unlike mine which is still damp and crooked. I turn.
The sheets move with me. Stand and go to the window, move the
curtains. Outside light is high and strong. People on the street.
Open the window a little. I can hear them, see them. Laughing,
walking, basking in the street, the sun... *Laura.*

You have woken up. Turn to you and you are blinking and
yawning at me. Smiling. *Buenos días.*

Buenos días.

Go and sit beside you. Reach and touch your hair. Stroke it. A
faint strand still wet with my saliva. You still blinking at the light.
You say it again, slower and through your smile. *Laurrra.*

Pull me down and I lie in front you, my back to your chest. You
have an arm around my body. Heat creases in the space between
us. I stare at the window. Can feel air coming in. Warm air of salt
and summer city. Your hand rubs my belly then passes along to
my wrist. You blindly rub my circle bruise. We lie for a long time.
Your rubbing hurts me softly.

It is becoming too hot. But I don't move. Neither do you. We
don't talk. I listen to the faint noise from the street.

Today you are going to help me.

Today, but later.

Right now, doze and sweat. Later we will get up and wash, eat,
dress. Inma will be out. We will walk out of the flat together,
beside each other. Our arms will brush sometimes and you will
look at me and smile. Sun will make us squint. We will be sweating
across the city, past the sea, over the bridge, past people that you
understand and I don‘t, gossiping and talking. Up the hill, and
then we will arrive at the flat and you will be looking and smiling at
me more and more, laughing softly. I will be less and less. I will be
looking at the dark porch, lifeless. The building still and sweltering
but cold in the hallway. We will enter, dead quiet, apart from you,

looking around and the sound of your smiles. I will walk ahead, panting with each step, and you will drag behind, looking at the chipped white paint, the shadows that fall through the stairwell. You will stop laughing for a moment and you will look at me straight in the eyes, just to make sure, absolutely sure, that I know he is not there, and I will stare straight back at you and say, softly. *Si, Estoy segura.*

Yes, I am secure. I am sure and secure and I will try to open the door whilst I stare at you and it will be locked. You will laugh more and look down. No mat. Look up, on tip-toes to reach the ledge around the top of the door. No key. We will both stare at the door and it will stay shut and locked. We will not talk, but go back down the stairs and walk around the building to where his windows look out. On this side of the building there will be only one window, slightly ajar. It will be his. His last window on the left. It is next to blank wall and it is two storeys high. There will be no drain to climb up, nothing but blank, unhelpful wall until the black glass of the windows. We will return and stand and stare at each other outside his apartment door.

You will still smiling but your laughter will waver. You will look around. I walk up the next flight of stairs. There will be no sound. There will be nothing there. Kick a doormat, look around. Waste some time. When I go back down the stairs you will not be there. I will go down. I will think that you have decided to leave. Maybe wait for me outside. But you will be looking around the building for a car park. There will be none. You will look at the front and see a grey tarmac gap. No cars. You will feel confident enough with this and you won't explain but you will stare me deep in the eyes again and take my wrist. I will feel your pressure on my bruises as you take me back up the stairs and there you will lift up the mat of the neighbour's flat and you will take a shining silver key and you will open their flat. There will be nobody there. You will look around and I will follow you and it will be a boring, dull flat. Oblivious to its neighbour. This flat will not be special, but it will have windows and you will open the last window on the left. You will begin to laugh softly again and I will laugh softly with you. You will reach out and before stretching out your arm you will look at me again and tell me to hold onto you. I will hold you and you will step up onto the ledge, step across the outside of the building, and for a moment in the heat and the nobody and the silence, you will stand between the windows in the air. Then you will disappear and be inside his flat. I will shut the window and leave. I will replace the key. I will wait. You will open the door and

I will be inside his empty flat.

It is siesta time. The flat is sleepy and warm. Dust floats through the sections of light that fall through the windows. Tidy. Lamp-head down. Empty modelling space. His notepad and charcoals neat on the floor where he prefers to stand or sit. Next to his chair. I sit on it. Warm here, from sunlight. Breathe and watch the space. Empty. The slack rope is looped through the window pane, without me. Look at the notepad. Charcoal fingerprints on the edges. Reach for it. Stop. Keep looking. My fingers curl back into my hand, retract.

You come to my side. Look at me. Look at the notepad.

You take it, open it. Look between me and the pages. You move around to face me. With a soft smile, turn pages.

Smile wavers. More pages.

You entirely drop the edges of the smile.

Look at me.

Your eyes are wide and smile creeps back to the very edges of your lips.

Stare at me.

Reach the end of the notepad, replace it, and look more at me. I am looking up at you. We wait for each other.

Your hand creeps towards me.

But it stops short.

Kitchen. There are
four apples
a peach with a black hole in it
stale milk – almost all gone
a yogurt.

Role of snuss containers, unopened in their plastic. Mint flavour. I have never smelt the smell of snus on you.

In a high cupboard a bottle of sherry with a sugary, sticky lid

Dust in the cupboards beside the plates and glasses
A canister of rich, smoky coffee
Frying pan half filled with oil on the stove.

Bathroom.
Cheap razors
Tidy
Small pile of flaky, pastel-coloured towels
Unloved slivers of soap by the sink and bath
Dust nestled in cracks between mirror and tiles,
tub and floor.
Curls of dust and skin together in the corners that you can only
see from up close.
No smell
No bathmat
Mirror unclean and black spots creeping up its sides.

In a cupboard in the main open space of the apartment.
Two crates
Art supplies
Empty stack of notepads
In the bottom crate. A pile of notebooks – used. I do not open
them. Leaf at their edges, smell their dusty, charcoal and pastel
smell. Do not open.

Bedroom.
Bed is made. Rough at the edges with clean, unscented sheets.
White
One pillow, to the side
One side table.
I sit on your bed. It is low to the ground. Underneath it there is
dust and a box.
On the side table. A lamp and round, plastic container of the
mint snuss. In the top of it are used, still-moist packets. Touch
them. Spit and tobacco smell. Your spit
Thumbed copy of *The Invisible Man*. Your name in pencil inside
the front page. Curling, difficult handwriting. There is one shelf,
opposite the wardrobe. Fat, heavy dictionaries of Dutch, French,

Spanish and English. *The Last of the Mohicans.*

The Comedians. All have your name inside the front page.

English Grammar book.

Large heavy book of published photographs. Solid in my hands. The paper cover crinkles and glistens between my fingers. Pages smell new. They are crisp and crunchy and untouched. Each page slowly turned gives a waft of newness. Waft of sterile bookshop, couch and coffee and peeling-off price tags. Crackle of new plastic bag. Each page is a different photograph of the world. Of steam clouding off muddy street stalls in India. Of uniformed boys in China. Of heat rolling over mud roads in Senegal. Of an exotic, long-feathered bird. Of an endless, white desert. Of a rain-sodden, enormous advert for Coca-Cola. Of a flock of long-necked white geese taking off from a marshland. The colours are rich and overpowering. Same smell of each page as I turn it. Your name is below a photograph. It is near the back.

It is a photo of a group of children. The sun is high overhead and each child carries the shadow of his large head as a black bib on his brown chest. The stomachs are pronounced with swollen belly buttons and the children wear bright shorts. Some have prominent ribcages that run like piano keys down their bodies. Some hold up their hands to show pale palms and to cast more shadows. Some stare into the camera. Some smile, some don't. A taller boy to the left hooks his hands on his hips and dips his head down and to the side. The white balls of his eyes stand out like the white reflections of the sunlight on his forehead and nose. He is not smiling. Some of the children wear thin strings around their necks. In the background there is heat and bushland. Sky is clear, crisp, blue. The children's legs are caked with mud that has dried. The varying shades of brown blend them to the ground that they stand on.

Few clothes in the wardrobe. All plain, sad colours.

No shoes

A pile of large boxes.

Inside one there is photographic equipment. Some is old. Cameras and lenses. Well-kept. Neatly arranged. There is a space at the top like a gap between teeth.

Another box, more equipment.

Last box at the bottom. Filled with papers. Legal papers. Magazines. Papers with headings from charities. *Médicins Sans Frontières*, *Oxfam*, Others written in Spanish, Dutch. Bills.

These charities paid you. For the services that you rendered.

Photographer.

More legal papers. Lists of seven-digit numbers on them.

Copy of a will. Your last name. The birthdate would make the deceased your father. You are the sole benefactor; no other name is mentioned.

Another one, with a woman's name. Your mother.

In the side table there are two drawers. Both filled with piles of photos. Some held together in small groups with elastic bands, some not. In the groups with elastic bands, the photos have seven-digit numbers on the backs of them. Amongst the unbound photos there are landscapes, strange and foreign.

Mountains

Desert

Tundra

Different huts

Houses on stilts

Mud wall, low squatting thatched roofs

Some exotic birds

Safari game

Groups of white people unloading lorries and planes

A zoomed-in photo of a baby elephant, muddy and sodden, his trunk raised, the underside of it pink and lush.

In the bound photos there are photos of wounds. Hands missing from ends of arms. Bloody and new or old and shrivelled. One group is a catalogue of dead bodies, lain out on tarpaulins. Each person with a slightly different shade of coffee skin. Some naked.

Some with many wounds
Some with just one large one.

Close-up shots of cuts curving through hair. So close that flaps of skin, shades of muscles and blood, are large and beautifully detailed.

Some groups have mostly bullet wounds
Some mostly knife

I open some piles and spread them around me on your bed. The colours of skin and blood, of mud and sky, are smeared and spread through each set of photos. The shades of skin and sky, ground and forest, all change in each group. The shades of the blood and insides, the whiteness of a visible bone.

Your job was to catalogue this. Record it.

War photographer.

How much did you earn per photo?

The box under the bed has a beautiful rug on top of it. It is threaded through with many colours. There is gold thread. Images of birds. In the box there is a thick clot of beads, tangled and as bright as the rug. More photos. These are of people. You have written Dutch names on the back and I can see you in your mother's face, but more in your father's. You have the same eyes. Hair. Stance. They are next to a house in the countryside. In the garden. In the house. Happy. Sometimes you are in the photos with one of them. Younger, more fat on you. A smile, sometimes. There are some photos with a girl and you.

You have your arm around her.
In front of the house
The same girl is in a tent against the backdrop of a desert,
Then in a dripping rainforest,
A hut.

Close up, laughing, wet hair, an enormous insect with orange legs in her hands.

Some more beads. String is broken and the beads are scattered through the photos. Red, orange and blue, heavy and smooth. I

42

touch one to my lips. It is refreshing cold

There are more papers. Your name. Name of a hospital with a blue cross on the top corner of each pages.

Envelope with the same blue crosses.

Photos of you inside.

I know it is you.

Your head is not visible.

Your torso

Arm

Back

Your map of scars but not scars yet. In the photos the wounds are fresh, scatters of cotton and tape around them. Arm. Photos and photos of your arm. In some of them, different hands hold it up. Your fingers are held extended.

Without the hands, the fingers curled

Your lustrous blood

Your body younger,

Tanned.

Healthy and riddled with marks and cuts, like the peach. Deep inside you is visible in the close-ups, your hair, your pores, your layers of body. Your healthy arm has tubes of blood and clear liquid coming from it. These photos are also cold, refreshing on my lips. I cannot understand what is written on the papers.

More beads

You, without wounds,

No girl.

You with a group, some with medical coats on. Eager. Lots of tents. A child, beautiful chocolate- coloured skin, stands in the middle. She is not smiling. Holds hands with a medical-coat.

The same group but without you. More children mingled amongst. Everywhere there is dust, blowing through all the photos.

At the bottom of the box there is a plain envelope. Inside there is another elastic band of photos. The first photo from this group is of two smooth, earthy legs. They are being spread open and held by light, peachy fingers that hold them from just above the ankle. The fingers fall off the sides of the photo, but they are there, insistent. Insisting on spreading the smooth brown legs so that the camera can see in between them. Legs are hairless and very thin, the knees prominent. Round knobs of knee bone shine under deeper-shaded knee skin. The legs are lying on a hospital gurney. The gurney is made of blue canvas, stained with blooming, dark blue stains. On the pubis bone and the thighs there are dark marks. Some match the shade of the knee skin. Some open into cuts, dark red and puckered. Some rise into swellings. The girl is too young to have any pubic hair.

Instead of pubic hair, the lips and clefts of the cunt are distorted and swollen. On the outside there is very dark skin and further in there is bright, sore skin. Yellow, thin pus makes strings over the sore skin from the opened, raped insides. Hole gapes. It is open, not taut like the legs and the fingers, relaxed. It is large, collapsed into itself and sagging down. Tired. Ribbons of fresh blood are seeping from the inside and from the cuts. Running on top of old blood and sometimes mixing with the pus. Further down between the legs there is shit, caked and sloppy. Some of it is on the gurney, leaving more stains. All the fresh fluids are bright and colourful. The dry, old blood has become dulled, shitty scabs with a gentle light dust blown over them. The dust is blown over the emaciated legs, the filthy blue gurney. As the new blood and pus comes down from the wounds it mixes and darkens with the dust. By the time it reaches the shit and the gurney it is as dark as the scabs and the skin on her knees.

The amount of cuts and bruises increases towards the centre of the photo, like constellations around a bright, bold star. Instead of a star there is her repeatedly violated cunt that is being held open so that it can be recorded in this photo. In the rest of the photos there are only girls. Almost all too young to have grown pubic hair. Most are close-ups, although in some of the photos you can see a chin, a stomach. Most of the legs are spread stiffly but some of the legs don't need to be held. These legs drape over the edges of the gurneys. These girls are covered with sheets that are peeled back only to expose the legs and cunts for the photographer. In these photos the sheet falls off and over the tops of the photos; they entirely cover the little bodies so that the girls would not be able to see or move or breathe. In one of these photos the folds of the sheet are filling up with the dust. It has blown over everything and rests in every crack that it can. Even the cracks on either side of her toe nails are gently being plugged up. On the back of these photos there are girls' names next to the catalogue numbers.

A catalogue for an assignment, for a job.

Catalogue numbers later written in bills. In reports.

I lie for a long time on top of the made bed. Have put everything away. Neat. Perfect as it was. An old snuss packet in my fingertips. Its wetness dries out in the summer air. Breathe in the mint-you-tobacco smell, more and more until I cannot smell it any longer. Don't sleep. Look at the ceiling, lonely string of cobweb in one corner. Lie for a long time. Starts to get dark outside.

I forgot that Bea was there with me. She has been sitting in your chair, half-asleep. We leave. Can barely see anything anymore in the flat and neither of us switches on a light. She takes my arm softly and leads me away, down the stairs and down the hill, the night covering everything very quickly so that soon, when I look back, I cannot see your empty flat.

Bea.

You are still leading me as we go down the hill. Different to walk down here with someone, with you. Still holding gentle onto my arm. We see the park. Chinese clothes shop. Restaurants. Roundabout. The old tobacco factory. Smell the river, the water. You smell it, too. You, quiet, and looking around. I don't know if you have been to this part of the city before. Fingers soft and warm, wrapped around my arm. Watch you out of the corner of my eye and it is at the bridge that your mouth shuts. Snap. Your eyes focus and you look at me. You watch me. No words. Full head turn and your jaw gapes again at me. Carry on, towards home. Still no sound. You just looking at me and me pretending that I don't know.

B ea.
Your grandmother gave birth in a building that had no door. The fast air bit and swallowed at your mother's head as it came forward, steaming red. Your Great-grandmother and the village midwife prepared, cutting and cleaning, the fatty baby for the arms of your grandmother. The hot water was boiled over the open fire and the burning smell hit your Grandmothers young, snot and tear-caked nostrils strongly; the smell of the fire would remind her always of the splitting of her body, production of your mother.

Your mother
grew up cold, loved and hungry. When she was twelve her menstruation began and her mother gave her kitchen rags. When she was thirteen, she was still hungry. A year later, breasts had developed ripe, grey-brown-big, against the undernourished town and the sunken jealous, undernourished girls who lived there with her. At fifteen, her brother, coming home drunk, groped her tits whilst she slept, leaving finger-print bruises. She woke up in the darkness, smelling siblings skinny smell and feeling the tenderness of her own skin. At sixteen, her cousin took her into the building that had no door when the family was all helping to slaughter the final cow and pushed her against a wall, pushing his hand into big breasts, another into his trousers and split open her legs whilst she stood. Afterwards, fluids dripped and mixing with the remnants of old fires and the cow had stopped making any sound. The family brought the dripping head, tongue lolling and you mother was made to sit, sticky head on knee, and extract the offal from the white jaw bones, smooth open spaces where brain had sat. When that final cow had disappeared and she had not eaten in three days, she went down to the mud-street at the bottom of the hill, walking very fast, behind the Mercado and into the salon of the town's brothel where a woman looked her up and down, asked her how many men she had had.

So your mother became a whore and your grandmother didn't say anything because your mother brought food up to the building

46

that had no door until, at seventeen, she began to live permanently on a small mattress in the salon of the brothel because she had tired of her cousin, and at eighteen, when even all if that began to leave her hungry, she travelled on foot with another girl who had a fresh and colourful winding scar on her abdomen, to a paved road behind the base of the foot-hills on which the village sat and they sat in a bus for the first time. Arriving in Rosario, they found a place and after several weeks of hard-work, your mother found that she was pregnant and that some men would pay more to fuck a pregnant girl until one night, she began to feel her first contractions and they did not stop until two mornings later when, heaving and heavy, she pushed you out and died before knowing what you were and what you are. The Madame dished you to an orphanage after attaching you to your mothers still-hot tits for your first milk and when you were growing, you were placed under the guidance of the eager nuns, not knowing and yet knowing that your mother had been a *puta* and that she had died by the grace of god just late enough to shove you out of her dirty body. At eighteen, full of holy education and an infection to spread what you knew, you joined a group heading to Europe in a boat, not a quick plane. You were coming to make contacts with churches. To spread the word of God. Once in Spain, arriving into the Bilbao docks, you stayed with the nuns, mostly on the floors of church halls until you awoke one night to see one of the old, straggly nuns dragging in a girl who had snuck out in the evening by herself. You knew that girl by her long, hazel hair and her thin, sloping back that the hair slipped down when she was washing it and after the old nun had smacked the girl around the head and body, you began to doubt and so you left alone, quickly and quietly, catching a bus like your mother had done once. And now you are here. You are here with me. You tell me your story and it is wonderful because you do not need words to tell it. You arrived here, you arrived here just like me and you were beautiful. You are beautiful.

I caught it.

This virus, like love.

Not sure exactly from whom, or when, because it can stay, dug deep inside the body, for hours, months, years. Forever.

It is a virus. There is no cure.

Waiting in the café for Marcos.

Sometimes love, the virus, never exposes itself.

I was persistent about the café as a meeting place. The weather outside beginning to turn.

Turning towards the last month of summer.

The café in the free art gallery with high, cool ceilings. The building proud, white, solid on the promenade. The paved promenade that resists the city on one side, the shops and the high buildings and the people. Resists the sea on the other side. An ornate handrail that falls into nothing but rough rocks, sand and ocean. Out in the bay, the tiny island with the trees and, almost hidden, the white, empty church, and then waves and waves and white foam and sea that stretches into the horizon.

It is hard to forget, because the pain of the first blisters between my legs was incomparable to anything in my life.

High, cool windows. Wind blowing away the light-grey sky, revealing dark blue. Rubbing at it like a thumb, rubbing away. Pushing all that sky into the opaque sea.

Can't remember why I insisted on it, this place, public, to meet.

The blisters had bloomed, bright yellow, curving through my legs and up, swelling the red, thick folds of intimate skin.

Trees shivering outside, leaves moving like waves. Wet, cool. Continuation of the dark, moving water out there in the ocean.

And walking had been painful. Urinating had been pain. Sharp, digging pain. Fingernails clenching, deep and hard.

Everything had hurt. It did not allow me to think about anything else. It arrested me.

This café is an open, empty space. Intricate turquoise tiles, plaster-cast details and dark, stony pillars jutting up through the room and amongst the toothpick-thin tables. There are not many people. It is quiet and it could be a café in any city, any country.

I remember the spindles of piss, running over the love ulcers.

Imagine the welts deep inside me where I can't see or touch, curling and lipping one another. Love was sorest at its most ripe. As soon as the scabs had crusted together, the sensation, the lucid and easy slopping of moistness changed into cracking, restrictive, full-bowels-bladder weight on dried blood patches. Couldn't move, breaking the delicate and intricate scabbing if I moved. Held down by this, my sickness, my body.

Mine.

Waiting and I have some more time for waiting because I am early. And looking inwards toward the city, cars are driving past outside. Black, moving windows.

All so clean, with my clothes to cover me. Waiting.

Nobody has to know. It can be a secret, covered up and quietly painful. Nobody needs to know anything. Nobody needs to know that I caught this love, this virus.

Catch.

Wonder if he is going to come and meet me, here, outside of the closed sweaty doors.

I should tell them, I know, I should talk about this evidence that I have found of love, this problem, straight away. Nip it in the bud, before it spreads. Don't know anything about them, don't know who he is with or how he spends most of his time.

Does he know where this café is? How well does he know the city. How well, like me, knowing where to put hands, in a pose. When to move. How to.

People enter and they are all Spanish because the winter is coming and blowing away all the tourists, the foreign faces all smudged out.

They drip in, rosy hairy Spanish people. They order *Cola Cao* and *café con leche*.

They eat Pintxo's because now it is late and hungry.

Cannot see anything out of that window now.

Don't know if he cares to come, but will see him again tomorrow, no matter what. In the cafe class. No avoiding.

Don't know where this came from, bursting open all over me. But I have an idea, have seen it before.

I am here, have stuck myself here, in Spain.

Still cannot say hardly anything, what have I been doing with my time? Catching and passing on viruses.

Is love a virus?

Are the blisters, these sores that have burst in the secret parts of my body, are they evidence of love? Are they evidence of intimacy? Can't I think about anything else? Can I feel anything else?

Don't know anything.

He doesn't walk through the door.

Never.

I sit here waiting. Dark turning day outside. And I remember where I have seen the ulcers before.

Not on me. On her.

It clicks. So stupid not to have realised before.

On Bea. She gave me this love.

If you walked away from the high ceilings, the coffee, the people, the café, outside. If you go out there, you are on the right hand side of the middle beach. The city has three beaches, the furthest to the right is separated from the others by a river mouth. Zurriola beach. On its furthest, right side there are very large rocks piled up to the malecon, a walkway which runs the length of all three beaches. The malecon ends here with a gate where there are fishermen and hobos. The gate leads to nowhere. After and back from the malecon, even further to the right, there is lush green hill, lonely houses scattered on it. The end of city. Behind and away from the ocean, alongside the hill, the malecon fattens out and becomes a car park, flat, smooth concrete where there are skaters, playground, shops, bars and then the city. If you stay with Malecon, look towards the water, look down. In the rocks there are wild cats, pregnant and scruffy. People, lovers, sitting on the ledge of concrete that crowns the rocks and makes the railing of the malecon. Watch the waves. The waves are big here. There are surfers, small and quick in the water, picking their waves and avoiding getting smacked in to the rocks and the cats. Occasionally the waves crash right up, black crabs and seaweed, white foam spattering the malecon and the lovers. Carry on walking around the malecon and you are beside the sand, still below you. Pass a club which looks out on onto the sea, where you heard that a tourist was stabbed to death at the end of the summer in a drunken fight. Carry on. Wooden posts sticking up from the sand below, the posts in neat rows, anchoring seats and umbrellas for rent. The Kursall, modern building made of light and angles. It sits, part of the sky on the corner of the beach, at night time it is entirely lit up with white-yellow light. It hold a jazz festival every year. Artificial rocks spread out in front of it to guide the river mouth into the open water. A pier goes with it. Follow it back in land and turn away from the Kursall.

Cross the bridge over the river. Stinging smell of salt and fish. Taste it on your lips. Avoid the tourists, flopping lazily between the beaches and the city. Cars. People on bikes. Traffic lights. Smooth paving stones. Go straight on and you are in the city, in the *Parte Vieja* or go at a right angle, then curve with the fat hill, the malecon squeezing around it and falling down into more enormous dark rocks and large, white waves. On the top of the hill there is a statue of Jesus and a small castle, rambling and broken, with green grass and weeds crawling over it, more wild cats. Calm and quiet. Down on the malecon, carry on, right around, go down some steps, pass the aquarium and look out onto the two remaining beaches that are to your right. La Concha, Ondarreta. The island in their bay. The crumbled hotel that sits, old and proud on the hill at the end of the Ondareta, marking the other end of the city and its beaches. At the end of Ondaretta Malecon and below the hotel hill there is tennis courts and the Peines del viento. The wind combs. They are large metal sculptures that comb the wind and are sodden by the waves that crash over them. From this final point of the malecon the island is close. When the tide is low the rocks between the mainland and the island almost make a path. Sharp brown, wet rocks. The Basques say that once a decomposed whale washed up, over these rocks and right onto the Ondarreta beach. Large white whale vertebrae with rotten white strings of flesh. Travelled for miles and miles.

Go right back round to the steps and the aquarium. Descend.

Here is the port. Large and small boats. More little steps down to the water. Large hunk of smooth round metal, jutting up from the paving slabs. People used to tie a large boat here. There are restaurants and tourists. The boating club building. Edge of the old town that meets you from around the other side of the hill. People. Keep going and you are at the terraced gardens where there are small birds, flying low and chirping, but only when it is sunny. The building, the public art gallery with the café, is here, the large, long windows. A merry-go-round that is faded pastel colours. When night falls, people walk here, lovers. People ready for fiesta. Drunk and dressed up. Carry on, along La Concha, the malecon here has a bike path, some trees, large, expensive apartments. Two grand, old hotels. Their terraces. Below the malecon there are two subterranean discos. Above, there are many restaurants. The sand gently slides into the calm sea to your right. Keep going. The road comes beside you on the left from the city and pushes into the malecon, making it thinner. Ornate handrails to guard you from the sand below. In the day, there are less people on this part of the beach. Rocks, a tunnel for the cars. Carry on and you are at Ondarreta again. You understand the curve of the coast here now. You go back, to where night is falling. Fiesta is beginning and the sky has become black. You cannot see the beach anymore, now there is no water, no island, just darkness, where the city slips into nothing.

I look at him as I take off my wet coat. Slow. T-shirt. No bra. All my clothes sodden through to damp skin. Outside there is bright-grey, wet light. Soft sound of the rain. Drop my skirt. I wait, next to the windows, standing in the normal space.

He is still not looking at me.

He is preparing his materials. The air inside is still, contrasts with the dripping windows. My panties are white-wet, see-through. Hair, a wet lump on my shoulders. Still. He is plucking charcoals and looking at something. Does not look at me as he moves to his seat and notebook. He has a deeper tan, extra wrinkle of dark skin under the eyes, than when I last saw him.

He looks up.

The eye wrinkles fall into purple V's under each row of eyelashes. Shirt has the two top buttons open. Chest hair. Shirt tails creased and loose against his trousers.

Stand tall and wait. Look into his eyes. He doesn't look back.

Take them off. Your pants.

I take them off. Move to drop them onto the other wet clothes, stuck together in a wet pile. He doesn't offer to dry them.

Body moist with rain. The scabbed sores in between my legs are sensitive to the air, the cold. I feel them. I feel my cunt sensitive as well. All stuck and moist together.

Sit down.

He is looking at me now. I sit. Slow. Careful. Legs still together. Remember the cold shiver of the floor.

No. He is concentrating even more now, as he speaks.

Legs apart. Knees bent in.

I spread my legs a little. Bend my knees. Pain is scabs opening between the legs. There is a sore directly in the crease on the top of my inner creases of skin, just above my cunt. I looked at it before, in my room, with a mirror. I feel as though it is that sore that splits a little. Pain makes me tense up inside myself. I lean forward with elbows on knees. It worsens the splitting and I wobble. Lean back. Rest on hands on floor.

He looks at me.

Looks at my body. Eyes moving slowly down. He does not speak. Sound of rain. I watch him. His face unmoved, cold. His left hand wafts slowly makes small circles, whilst the other grips a pencil. Eventually, the circles slow. Look closely and see his fingers that grip the pencil relaxing and tensing. His eyes have stopped between my legs. They stare and stare. Grip and relax. Stare. Grip. Relax.

We stare for a long time.

The cold day is reaching deeper and deeper into me, spreading all down my back, my spine.

His eyes illuminate.

They are torches again. Warming the pain around my cunt. The

53

heat goes inside me. Feels like the beginning of sticky, special heat. On the outside, cunt is confusing shivers of the outer cold and the inside warmth, and of pain, of him staring. Not speaking still.

He drops the pencil.

It tinkles on the floor. Stands. Steps towards me. The air moves between us. He stops when he is halfway here.

Spread your legs more. Flatten them.

He is looming tall. I continue to look up at him and the pain of the splitting, ulcered skin is already bright hot as I begin to flatten my legs.

Spread.

His voice stern. Small step closer and the light dropping silent from his face.

I want to obey. I try. The pain is unbearable. The increase of contact with the floor is puckering-up cold on the exposed skin.

I cannot. Pain unbearable. Try again and freeze at the ripping feeling.

He steps closer. His feet level with mine. Dark shadow, he is. Sick feeling takes over from the heat, the wetness and the cold inside me. His foot flickers towards mine. Then it quickly returns. Nausea washes down through me. My neck cranked and tight to look up at him. He steps over my legs. His bitter, unwashed smell brushes me, his left arm trembling now. He is standing facing the window. Next to the shadows on his back, the rainy daylight is stark and cold. I look outside at the light, and at his dark back, and at the movement of his left hand, taking something that I know from the window handle.

The cord.

He comes back and kneels behind me.

The unwashed smell is masculine. Yanks my hands together with his right hand. My lungs stretch out and open. My weight, unbalanced, falls onto my straightened, together arms. Pain in my shoulder blades, like breaking might feel. I pull my weight forward with my buttocks and my cunt hurts so much. I can feel how near he is to me. His breath on my skin. Can hear, through the sound of the rain, the sound of his breath. Fast. He pinches one wrist with his little finger and I can feel him working the cord around first one then the other wrist with his thumb and index finger.

54

Memory of the old bruises comes back. My breaths are quick, stretched. He ties them so that the wrists touch and I can splay my fingers out.

I reach my fingers out soft into the air. There is nothing. I extend them straight, stretch them.

Feel a knee, hard. Material is warm, dry. Say nothing. His breath, hot on my shoulder. Sound of his saliva. He keeps pulling the wrists tight. Each jolt rocks my weight over the ulcers. Each one echoes through the pit of sickness that I feel inside me. He must be almost finished. My fingers softly reach again, to the side. My left middle finger brushes something. It is a fingertip. It is quivering. Soft pad of skin. Dry and warm. Sickness and feeling wet all over and wanting to spread my legs for him all mixes. Push more with my fingertip. Feel more connection, the fingertip's soft skin giving to mine.

Break in his breath. He jerks back. My weight is unbalanced and my palms smack into the ground. Cry out with the weight rocking over me.

Cry out.

Making a searing, splitting feeling. I try so hard to swallow the cry but it slips out. Am stuck now, cannot move the weight from my palms. Cold has snapped in, sudden, taken over me entirely, through every bone and part of flesh. Cold and sick. He is above me, still behind. Steps back around. I look up at where his shirt is open. Hair and skin. Dirty, dry skin. He stares into my eyes.

His foot flickers again.

This time, it touches mine. The toe of his shoe against the arch of my foot.

Spread.

He speaks stern. At the same time, the toe of his shoe pushes me apart.

This time, the cry falters and blocks my throat. It sits, fat and sharp, beneath my mouth and stifles my breath. The pain inside me has burst bright open, a firework. Slow motion. Slow, it passes up in me, blocks my throat. I blink black and blink open to the burst light. Blink black. Blink him, light. Blink black.

Black out.

First thing
that I feel is
sharpness in my shoulder blades.

They prop up my weight.

Flat, strained palms against the floor. The pain is strong between the legs, but unwavering. It is bearable like that. I can breathe, re-feel my open lungs. Breath beating fast in and out of them. Click. The cold is strong, but unwavering. It is bearable like that. Can hear the rain. Can hear a clicking sound.

I cannot see.

Click.

The pressure of the material tied over my eyes pinches the top of my ears. It smells of his things. His clothes. Him.

I slide my palm along the floor to one side. The cord has been loosened. Rock my weight slightly forward and back onto one wrist. Pull the cord with the other wrist. Know that I am still tied together. But I can move. I can raise my wrist and bring it almost to my waist, then it is taut and pulling my other wrist out from underneath me, making my elbow buckle. Click. As I test the cord, the shift in my body pulls at the pain and tenses my stomach. I begin to open my mouth. I cannot sense where he is. If he is there at all. If he is the clicking sound.

Click.

My mouth is dry. Raspy tongue, taste iron. Swallow changes nothing. No saliva. Dried out.

Lips feel themselves open. Nothing in there, nothing to mouth out.

Do not cry.

I am photographing you.

He is close, in front of me. Very close.

My breath holds my lips open. It beats and beats. Slow. Put my weight back between both wrists. Palm slips. Elbow and forearm bang the floor. Air slams out of my mouth. Vertebrae are stretched out. Head falls back and cracks my neck. Dizzy.

Try again.

Put my weight back, feel equal.

There is sweat, my sweat.

Feet slip. Pain in the middle of it all. He is watching me. I can feel it.

Click.

The sweat making me slip. It appears quick. Cold and clammy on hands and feet.

I regain balance. Legs bent up, still spread apart. Stomach flops in and out with breath. Open mouth. It is wet now. It is full of saliva. Full and need to swallow it back before it blocks off the air that I suck in.

I don't move.

Saliva filled. Swallow and don't move and regain breathing.

The clicking pauses. Footsteps come towards me. His smell, his sense. He hooks his shoe in the crease of my knee and lifts slightly. His shoelaces press soft into the flesh as he takes its weight for a moment.

Takes the shoe away, quick. Leg smacks flat on ground. Click. Click.

Move.

Slow. Do not cry out. Straighten out the other leg. Extend it into the pain. Extend the spine and arch it. Move around. Work with what I can do, without crying. Sicking up the feelings in me. Don't want to cry. Click. Click.

Sicky spit and swallow in my mouth.

Good.

His voice is further away now. In the darkness, the tone of his voice is rich and smooth. Try to keep making movements. Move as far as I can. I think about nothing, my mind dark inside. Feel again, the heat slightly inside me, the dampness, all in my cunt. Try to spread as far as I can, bend the knees a little. Palms at the side of my buttocks. Cord taut, stopping me. Pain constant. Jabbing with the splitting in between me.

Cold sweats re-bloom.

Good.

Hear that he is nearer.

The feeling of the splitting mixes with the new fluids in between my legs. Twitching, expectant, sickly feelings, all there, all blooming open.

Click.

Bask in this a moment. Good.

Clicking pauses again. Sound of something on the ground. Footsteps.

He is coming closer. His presence twitches me more inside. The cracked, broken scabs, moistening in his air. Sound of his kneeling behind. Masculine, earthy smell. Lack of his fingers against my skin as they pull the cord, yanking my wrists. His breath, quicker than before. Quicker than when we were last in this position. Wait and feel for a finger to touch my wrist flesh.

It doesn't. The cord falls with a final, deft pull. Untied.

We do not move for a moment. I see as though it is his shadow that covers my sight. The shadow that I have seen before, beside the window, blocking out the day. Covering it and me. The shadow that I can feel, that can dry out the rain.

Moments, more and more.

My heart a thick, wet beat. His fast breath. Slip my hands and sweat out slow from my side. They keep my weight. He stands. The wave of his heat and smell passes over me, from my cold buttocks on the floor, my spine, nub of my neck, to the parting of hair on my head. His presence moves on, steps away. Same sound of object from the floor. When he speaks he is passing in front of me. Dark light moving on my eyes.

Get up.

I can already imagine the feeling of standing up. I do not want to.

I obey. I put my weight forward and to one side. Lift the opposite hand and go to push my weight onto my feet and lift my buttocks. No balance. Smack back onto my buttocks.

Smack.

Click.

Jar my spine. Bright light, like his headlights, blooms in front of my eyes. Splitting again,

Breathe.

There is a spit of acid in my throat. It bubbles up to my mouth and then falls back down. As it retreats, there is a sob there in the throat. It racks out. The sound is like gasping for breath. An animal sound. More of them come, rhythmic. The light subsides to the blackness again.

I put my weight to one side. Side of legs. Grind my knee into the ground. Twist. Click. Twist the pain around. It mashes and touches, moist and open-sore. I am on all fours. Hang my body and head down. The sobs make a softer sound. There is so much saliva in my mouth. Liquid in my nose and on the material over my eyes. It blots out the smell of him.

Click.

From here, the flexing of my legs makes the pain the tightest it has been. It is stretched now, right down to the bones of my knees. Balls of my feet against the cold ground. My body rises slowly. Hands off the ground.

Click.

Smack.

The bright light, brighter than before. Same spit of acid. Pain brightest and overwhelming.

It cuts out.

Sobs are knocked out, steady and loud. There is no more feeling. *Good.*

His voice is smooth. He is very close. Click. Reminds me that there is that flicker, there still, warm up in my cunt. Gasp. I am on all fours again. Click. My ribs heave. Spread my feet further apart. Take away my hands. Crouch. Stand.

Sobs do not stop. They heave with the ribs and the breath. Click. A new sweat breaks on the panel of skin between my breasts. I feel it blushing in my cheeks, my back. Click. I reach out with my hands. They find balance. I reach and shift my weight a little. My hands reach towards my ears, but they stop. Click. They fall to the sides of my body. My weight falls with them. It hangs over my ribs. The sobs, the acid sick taste, the sweat sheens cold over me. Click. Breathe. Breathe. His footsteps. It is difficult to breathe. Drops of liquid on the insides of my legs. Warm, fast drips.

Click.

The clicking sounds are slowing.

My breath heavy. It weighs me down with each sob and suck in of air. Heave.

Good.

He is very close. Behind me. There is a soft sigh of air as he sounds the d. It is sound of satisfaction. Sound of the object, the camera, on the floor. Hear his breath. Feel the large buff of heat from his body next to mine. That male smell. Mingled with sweat now. His presence a shadow over my already dark eyes. Coming closer and closer until his fingers – they touch me, my hair.

His warm, strong fingers.

And my whole body is hanging from my ribs. Heaving. Hanging on the beat of the heart. I lean my head slightly into those fingers. They catch my hair along with the material. The pain that cut out returns to me with each heave. The pain is in the ankles, the wrists, the knees and the loosened ulcers. Imagine the scabs all soaked and swallowed up, useless. Red, raw virus. With each push of air from my lungs, resistance from the panel of my chest and throat increases, as my weight pulls down against my escaping breath. Beating is stronger, heavier. His finger and thumb pinch one end of the material and a chunk of my hair taut. With the other fingers, he works loose the other end of the material. I do not know where is his other hand. It must float behind. It does not make contact with me. The material loosens a little. Fingers still fumbling. I push my head more into his fingers. Pull in more air. Sweaty air. Material falls a little. It covers my nose. Still dark. Dark with his shadow and the blindfold. Open my mouth wide. It unsticks inside with spit, lips uncrack at their edges. Suck in air. He yanks at my hair. Sound of air hissing into me. Hissing with the hanging beat of my heart. Air.

Material falls down again, further down my face. Light floods in. Shut my eyes. Want to breathe. There is not enough air. Instead, my mouth sucks in material, wet with salt. No air, material. Open eyes again. The light is white bright and there is no more rain outside. Whitest bright. Sucking sound. Swelling heart. Heave, again and again. Swelling beats hot in the chest. There is no air in me. Ugly, ugly sound. Faster and faster beats of heart, searching.

He pulls the material away. Tight feeling of hair tearing.

It is too late. The beat is continuous.

I am already falling.

Knees bounce hard off the floor. Brightest light. Dark again. No rain. No beat. Dark black.

I see thighs.

The white skin of them, in the white light.

No sound of rain anymore.

The blonde, small hairs covering them, the tops of bluish knees, prominent knee caps.

Squinty white light it is.

Quiet hangs in the still air. Heavy.

Stillness presses on my body. On my tired hips. Sunken waist. Hip bone crunched against that hard floor. White thigh flesh.

Curled up, I am. Foetal and uncomfortable.

No sound but quiet, cold breath. My breath.

Inner thighs are damp where they stick together. Drying liquid in between them is discoloured.

Eyes begin to focus easier.

Thigh liquid is not my sticky, sweet sex. It is as thin as water. It is blood and ammonia smell of piss that I could no longer control. It is dark and staining on the bloodless, cold thighs.

The thighs in front of my eyes. Skull, I rock it, left, right, squashing my ear into the floor. Left, right. Thighs, white and blue and discoloured sticky.

Roll my head. Squash ear. Gentle movement.

Each blink is clearer and clearer. The side of my body cold, touching the floor.

My breath is calm. It doesn't heave at all, not like before. Calm and cold.

Before.

Face scratchy with salt.

The light almost normal again in my eyes.

Push fingers under the cold, squashed ear on the rocking floor.

I lean up on my forearm. I can balance. Breathe. Can feel aches throughout my body.

Kneel. Slow, take my time to get there. Legs tight together, holding in the biggest ache there, solid held tight between thighs sticky.

His studio is sleepy and still.

Outside is sleepy and still. The rain has been switched off and everything is dreaming in its own siesta.

Kneel towards my clothes. Use my hands. Keep the legs as close as I can. Slide-kneel over the wooden floor. Through the sleepy light. Blinking and aching.

Clothes are still a sodden pile.

Beside them, a dry white shirt.

Take it in my hands. It is unstained, a clean white. It smells of the masculine smell. Think about what makes this smell.

Snus.

Him.

Dust.

His sweat.

Smell it in for a long time. Cover my face. My eyes. Make everything black. A lulling, sleepy black.

I am tired.

Exhausted. Throughout my body. My mind.

There is an envelope. A glass of water. Thirsty. Drink it all. Unsticks my throat.

I stand up.

All of a sudden. Rip in the legs and unstuck pain. Standing. Rush of blood to the head.

Easier than I thought.

I look around the entire room. Nobody. Everything seems normal. Camera discarded on his seat. Notebook, pencils and charcoals. Inanimate.

Go towards the kitchen, the tap. Pad, pad , pad of my feet. Wooden floor. Glass in my hand. Fill it. Drink it all. His name comes to my mouth, to call him. I don't. Breathe. Go back to where I had blacked out, near the window. Pad, pad, pad of my feet. Small steps. Sticky every time my thighs touch. Breathe. Breathe in his shirt.

Be very still.
Look out the window.
Silence. Shut my eyes.
Breathe. Silence.
Breathe in.

B ea.
You walk across the bridge between the Kursall and the old town. You look out at the ocean and the tide rising up into the river mouth. You smell the fish smell at the corner. Fish, salt, sea smell. You stand next to the fat, ornate post and breathe in the smell.

You have a choice. You could walk around the hill, to your right, in between the ocean and the hill with the Jesus statue and the stray cats. Or you could go straight on and cross along the other side of the old town, next to the rest of the city. There are a lot of people in the old town. You stroke the dirty paint of the enormous post. Night is falling, gentle and warm. People. Tourists. Everywhere.

You decide, and you begin to walk through the people. Walk deeper into them; some of them are eating ice cream, drinking. Eating. Enjoying holidays. Unhurried. Walking. Standing in groups. Waiting. A lot of different people. You hear their different languages; Portuguese, Basque, English, which makes you think of me, Spanish. Lots of Spanish accents. You hear accents from home and you think about how much you do not want to be there, ever again. You walk up the shallow steps to skirt the edge of the main crowd between you and the buildings of the old town. To the other side of you, there are the little patches of grass and trees and bike stands that separate the old town from a large road and then the rest of the city.

You have crossed almost all of that side of the old town whilst

63

you have been deep in thought, thinking of home. You are happy, relieved, here in Spain and by the ocean. Surrounded by people. By a more pleasant, lazy sun. You pass the free art gallery. In the stone walls are many holes. You know that they are from bullets. From the guns of protestors. You have seen the people protesting here in the city. They speak a language that you didn't even know existed, until you arrived here and at Bilbao, and saw the strange, foreign graffiti. The protestors are very passionate and angry. They protest every Saturday. Police wearing riot protection keep them together in a group. You do not understand what they are saying, their strange Basque language, but you like to watch them. You think about me again, briefly. You understand me and the protestors in the same way – by not relying on language.

You are at the side of the art gallery building now, on the promenade next to the merry-go-round and the small garden where the birds sing and fly low when it is not raining. Night has just dropped down over everything. You feel as though you have just missed seeing it, just missed the light disappearing. Warm, and dark out in the bay. You walk along the malecon. Already there are groups of people who walk and talk drunkenly. They are many different ages. There are couples too, and some people, like you, that walk around alone. Some hurry and some take their time. You see the lights of the large, sea-front hotels, the bars and the restaurants. You walk until the malecon is a thin strip between these hotels, the cycle track, occasional small trees, and the ornate railings that hold you in from the beach below. You sit down on a bench next to a little tree. There is bird-shit on the bench. You look at it, wet and white and black. You sit next to it. Watch people for a while.

There is a group of young girls in front of you. They chat and look over the railings and at each other. Two of them look around frequently at the other people on the malecon. They have bottles of alcohol that they pass between them. They are talking about somebody's boyfriend and where they are going to go tonight. The two that are more curious smile at each other. They show their teeth, like dogs. When they smile at the passers-by, their lips are squeezed shut over the teeth. One of them looks at you. She shows her teeth. You smile back and look around you. A man is sitting on the other side of the bird-shit. He is talking on his phone, quietly. You cannot hear what he says. You look at the girls. One of them throws an empty bottle towards the black ocean. It is high and visible in the air for a moment. Then gone. They all watch the bottle and then carry on talking. Argentina. You will never go back. Looking out at that ocean, you know that you won't. Those nuns. Some of the other girls in the orphanage felt the same as you. You know they did. They didn't talk about it very much, but you could see it in their eyes. In their pursed lips. Your open, crying lips when that young nun who had a birthmark squatting on her eyebrow, staring at you, told you that it was in your blood. To clean yourself and go and beg God for forgiveness of your mother and yourself and your dirty, dirty sins. Beg him and beg him until you cannot beg anymore. They did not take you to the hospital or the doctor that first time that it appeared. You went to her and stared above her eyebrow, whilst she looked between your legs. She said nothing at first, just dragged you to the bathroom. She made you cry. You opened your beautiful mouth and cried. Pain had been so strong. She told you that you were *bueno para nada.*

Then, the man is not on his phone. He has thick grey hair. A matching moustache. Tan. Suit. He looks at you. You look. You turn your lips up to smile as you turn your eyes away. There is a terrace near to you. It is marked by large white umbrellas and the waiter has to cross the cycle track to return to the hotel. He is waiting as a slow cyclist passes him. Tray full of drinks. It rests on his shoulder. Immaculate white cloth draping over the edge of it, under the drinks. The man next to you talks in your direction. He asks you if you would like to drink something with him. You look back at him. You have never drunk in a nice place before. You think about what it might be like for a moment, and you are curious. You say yes. He looks at you for a long moment and says nothing. Then he opens his arm out from his side and gestures at the terrace. He is staying in this hotel. He has a tab that they can use. You stand up and look at the girls and the bird-shit and more people, swaying gently along around you, and you feel him put his hand, very soft, on your back. You walk to the terrace next to him. Sit down. There are two layers of tablecloths, clean, like the waiter's tray-cloth. The same waiter comes to the table and the man orders something from him. When the waiter has left, the man asks you how long have you been in Spain and if you like it. He likes Argentina. He likes your accent. You look after the waiter, crossing the cycle track. His tray has dirty glasses on it now. You look the man straight in the eyes and tell him that you do not like Argentina and that you have not been in Spain very long. You look at the wrinkles in the tanned skin and the soft lip of his shirt collar. You look at where the girls had stood beside the railings, but they are gone. You cannot see where they went. The waiter places a drink in front of you. He leaves. The man tells you that you are beautiful. And in the same sentence asks you if you like your drink. You taste it. Taste is strong and bitter and you cough a little. He echoes your cough with a bark of laughter. You both watch the people walking by. His phone rings. He talks on it again, quietly. You drink in doses and watch him. It is different to the alcohol that you have tried before. He is looking at the dark bay. His free hand strokes his cheek slow. He drops that free hand below the table so that you can't see it. Straight away, you feel his fingers. They search and find your knee and touch it gently. Takes his hand away. Then returns it, and without moving his body very far, reaches a little up your leg. You look down and then at him. He is still talking. When he finishes his call, he pushes his drink to one side and looks at you. You look back. His eyes are brown. He tells you that his hotel room is number 415. He takes a key from his pocket and tells you to go there.

You go.

You look out of the window at the ocean. With the moonlight and the weak light from the city, you can see the little island and the nothing of the horizon. You look around you. Seaview, double room. He is still lying on the bed. He has opened the drawer of his side table and taken out some notes of money. You heard him do it while you looked down, watched people, staggering now, along the malecon. He gestures towards

66

you. You step over to him. He passes the notes to you. He asks if you have a phone number. You say no. He asks how much would you require to return in four hours and sleep here with him. Tells you that he would require you until 9.30 in the morning. You look at him, straight into the brown, nameless eyes. Don't hesitate at all. You name your price.

Awake. Alone. In one sudden snap, I am both. White morning in my still-damp, still-broken bedroom. Awake. Alone. Still feel my knees. They are two round, hard bruises. She is not here. Old pillow smell of our hair. No Bea. No sound of rain. Soft light of sun in the curtains. Open window. Air. That air that I have only smelt here. That salt, city, clean air. It is with me now. Now it is the air of my yawn and breath as I stretch. Roll over the knees. Eyes are one blink and used to the light. Cool space beside me that I move into. Sheets billow and slip back, touching all over. Heavy armpit stench. My hands touching the wall. Stretch. Curl up. Smooth, wet skin between my legs slips against itself. The virus has dug deeper. No ulcers anymore; it hides inside me for a while. Think about pissing, now without pain. Moving. All with a healthy ignorance because there is no pain. No ulcers. My empty bed. Sandy, soft light. Clothes in a pile on the floor. I remember eating cherries. Spitting pips out of the window at the street and café people sitting down below. Damp leaves lie in the drains, but no rain. No nothing. Lush. Ready. What's not there? First her, then him. Always in the end him. What are his mornings? Dresses himself with one hand. My toe touching cold wood of bed frame. I am falling and it is raining all around. Rain is warm. So comfortable. Delicious shiver falling back into sleep you are again...

Awake again. I am alone. Later. I must have fallen back to sleep. No Bea. Need to go to the toilet. I go. Sound of my feet clapping on wood floor. Piss and no pain, no ulcers, no nothing. Afterwards, shower away dirtiness and I dry myself in the sunlight of my room. Dress myself. Opened curtains. I smell of city clean. Ready. Eat. Recall waking and falling back into sleep in the

early morning. Cherries. I eat fruit and some juice for breakfast.
Sit again, look out. Squint out at the sun-city. Milk-blue day.
Clothes, like the sheets I felt on my body in bed. Before. It was
this morning again. I have not seen Inma yet. There is no Bea
anywhere. I look into her room. It is bright opaque as my room.

I leave the flat.

The street is familiar Spanish sounds and a bright, blooming,
red parasol of a shrivelled old senora. The day is as hot as broad
summer. Suck in that white air. Walk. Not fast, not slow. Cross the
bridge. Taste salt on my lips. Low tide. See the sludge-green rocks.
They shine up at me from the sides of the river. Water dribbles
back to the sea. Up. Carry on walking. Shut your eyes and walk.
Almost into the cycle track. Dog shit. Keep going. First spread of
sweat. Begins on forehead. Keep going. Tongue made of sponge.
Rubs bridge of my mouth. Slow, it surfaces and then flops back
down between my teeth. Did not brush them. They have slime
on them. Explore this with tongue. Walk past a lot of shops. The
tree smell. Cool air touches me from the park. The Tabakalera.
No huge strips of posters anymore hanging from the walls. The
windows dark or broken. Building big, imposing, beautiful. The
hill. Long. Always longer than I think. Sweat in the dark armpits
now. Trees, quiet. I am at the gate. More windows like dark, open
eyes. Hot air from them. No people on the street. No cherry pips
here.
   Knock. You come quick to the door. You. You stare at me,
staring at you. Fully dressed. Neat. What I see of the apartment
is neat also. We stand for a while. Do not speak. Your right hand
comes straight out in a line and attaches to the open door. You
left hand wavers beside you, coming forward sometimes to quiver
between us. The light comes mostly from your open door, out into
the hallway. It brings my attention inside, to where the light comes
from. Where everything looks bright.
   You lips part a little. You breathe in between them. When your
words come out, they are small and soft. Hazy mixing with the
light beams around you.
   I didn't give you another appointment to come here.

The open door. No rain.

I have no answer. Shift my weight. Maintain eye contact.

Several more silences, piling into one another. His left hand reaches gently out.

My eyes follow the movement. The fingers loose in their joints, flopping. My gaze meets, touches, the fingertips

I lean in a little.

Move my eyes.

The hand retreats, shivering.

You need to give me a moment to prepare.

Right hand lets go. The door flaps entirely open. He steps aside. I walk in. It is a good time of the day – that light is covering the floor, the modelling space. It will light me up.

I go to the space beside the window. The cord is not attached to the window anymore. It is a knot in the corner. I take it, unravel it. Thread it through the metal of the window. Make the end into a loop, stuff it through the gap. I take off my clothes. He carries in charcoals. A notebook. His chair is already there. He brings in his camera. Each item arrives, deliberate and individually in his right hand. I am almost naked. Remove my socks. Panties. Move my hair behind my shoulders. Pull the loose strands from my chest and throat, drag them together with fingertips. Sit down. He is in the bedroom. I hear him moving in there, but I cannot see him from where I sit. Bones under my buttocks crack against the hard floor. Hear the opening creak of a door. I stretch, open and close the bones of my spine. Listen to his sounds. Twist myself around, feeling warmth of muscles moving inside me. Hard floor.

His sounds stop.

I stop too. Listen for him, but there is nothing. No sound.

Hazy light. Still day.

Use my hands, my fingers, to shift myself along the floorboards. My wrists make 90 degree angles to that hard floor. Shift and slide my buttocks, feet, move slow and silent towards his bedroom silence.

A rustle of papers.

I stand up, neat, quick. In one jump. Step silent on the balls of my feet.

Reach the point where I can see the edge of what is inside the
bedroom. He does not notice me. I creep more. I can see his
bed, his wardrobe, his shelf. He is next to the wardrobe. Looking
down into something in his right hand. His left hand shakes beside
him. It makes his entire left arm and shoulder shake. He does not
seem to notice his body moving. He does not notice me. His neck
cranes down towards his hand. His breath is audible, heavy. I hear
it. It is the only thing that I hear.

I watch him for long moments. On the bed there is the lid of a
box.

I remember.

The same colour as that box under the bed.

Silent, I turn my body. Slide my feet back. My breath quick
and heavy. Now the tingle of sweat in my palms and under my
feet, greasing them along as I return to the space beside the
window. Drop my body to the floor. Buttock bones remember the
floorboards. I wait under the dangling ends of the cord. The light
bathes me all over, except the spine, which I press into the covered
panel at the bottom of the window pane.

I open my legs. Right open.

Hands beside buttocks. Press into them until there is the 90
degree feeling again.

Stretch open spine full. Wait.

He takes a long time to return to the room. His eyes look ahead
of him to where he is about to step. Still shaking arm. His bare
feet slopping on the floor with each step. I search to meet his gaze.

I find it. I find his gaze.

His breath has stayed the same. Fast. We suck in air with the
same rhythm. Our eyes stuck together. He stands still, also bathed
in the sunlight. He is between the bedroom door and me. Skin
glints on his forehead. His eyes break away. He moves past me.
Feel the air move around him. He moves toward his seat. Eyes fall
right down. He sits. Sound of chair's feet moving on the wood.
Sharp squeak sounds. Reaches down. His clothes crumpling
around his movements. Shirt creasing into dark lines in his elbow,
his waist as he bends. Takes his paper and charcoals in his hand.
He looks at me, all over. I have not moved. Takes his time. My
eyes wait for his eye contact again. Warp of the sheets of paper

settling in his lap. Fast breath. Hold my pose. His lip moving a little, left arm quivering. Suck in of breath. Eyes on floor between us. He puts down the paper and charcoals. Creases of clothing. Stands. Squeak of chair. Takes a step towards me. His eyes advance. They reach my feet and continue. Again, eyes all over me.

Another step.

Another.

He reaches me. My neck cranked back, I look upwards. I find his waist, hand, shirt, crinkles, shoulders, hair, nape of neck, then eyes. He drops them down and looks at my body. I study his face. Lines on his forehead. Muted stains of purple under each eye. Stubble. His smooth, neat earlobes. Lips. Firm shut. That neck, nape, strong. Planted in the wide shoulders. His smell, smell his smell. Familiar. Look for an imbalance between his shoulders, his arms. I cannot see it.

His foot moves out.

His eyes pin down mine quick. Foot. Flicks against mine. Swish of his skin against mine. Naked feet. He pushes. I let him push. He opens my leg.

Wide.

Puts his toes under my ankle.

I feel the hair and nails and warmth of him against me. He lifts my ankle up.

Limp, I am.

Lifts it right up.

Removes his toes.

Our gaze intact. My heel hits the floor. Do not flinch.

Dull bang of bone under skin hitting wood. Let the pain wash right through me. Do not look away.

He is still. Looking all over me. I look straight back at him.

I leave my legs open. Wide open.

Wait.

As he returns to his chair. Left arm gentle. His back. Back of his head. Unkempt hair.

His clothes creased down his entire body.

Pose. Push my body forward. Push into my planted heels. Spread my fingers into the floor.

71

He sits. Takes up again his pad and charcoals. Warp of paper. Opens a page. Fingers go quick, flicking over the sheet. His eyes harden.

His fingers tense and curl with the charcoals. His eyes spread and move over me. Feel again my breath, quick and jumpy in my ribcage, my throat. The sweat spreads from the tips of my fingers, the pads of my feet.

It blooms in the bent cusps of knees.

In dark armpits.

In between my thighs.

The cool of removing my clothes, feeling air on skin. It recedes like the shadow from the midday room. His eyes light up as he draws.

The warmth spreads over me.

Warmth of his eyes.

Flick of a sheet of paper.

Saliva fills the sides of my mouth. Acidy slime of dirty teeth. Swallow wet.

Scratch of the charcoals over the paper. His eyes, narrowing and concentrating, falling all over me. I move with his eyes, they tell me where to go. I move for them. Times passes beside us. My eyes half burning in the white daylight, slices of sun pass through the windows and illuminate the dust between us. The sweat on my palms and in the creases of my body oils my movements.

The old warmth in between my legs is there again. His eyes touch it, clean, no virus, supple cunt, feel it slipping between my legs. My legs open and posing, head snappable, right back on my neck. Lean on elbows and crunch the bones until they hurt in the ground, but relax weight into them. Relax into the pain and suck up the chalky sounds of his fingers. Moving over me.

Next.

Reach up and hold the window pane. Use it to pull my torso up. Strain shoulders. Hands. Flop leave legs spread and cunt sticky sweet for him, now pull my wrists together under fingers holding the bar of the window. He watches me. No scratchy sounds from him or drawing.

72

He watches.

Me.

Heat between my fingers and feet.

Slipping slow on the floor.

His right side of body a line of thin shadow all the way down from his skull to his feet, where the light is not catching him from the window. The rest of his body illuminated, caught. The dark line on him catching the edge of his eye, his lips, his arm. It echoes the shadows that hide in the corners of objects in the room. They do not grow, those shadows. Do not reach out to cover him. Do not reach out to me. They stay in the corners. The light reflects the whites of his eyes and glisten of lips. Sweat on cheeks and forehead.

Slices of sun pass between us.

He is close now. He is dazzling.

His hand reaches out of this shadow line.

It is softer and moist on my wrists. His eyes right in mine. They feel right inside. Whites soft and glittering and so close that I could reach out and touch him. He holds my wrists between two fingers. Binds them with thumb and middle finger. The cord. Pliant, used. Holding and binding and when you are finished, you hold on for longer. Fingers.

You kneel. On your knees, you are between my feet, higher than me because I sit on my buttocks. Your entire body passes before my eyes as you neat, quick. Kneel. Your chest in front of my face as you finish binding my wrists with the cord.

Close. Your chest. Summer heat of you.

Your smell. It is the smell of your shirt that I have not brought back, of snuss and sweet sweat, man, hair in the dip of your throat.

You have finished binding. You sit back a little onto your heels. Do not remove your hands.

Presence dazzling, right there, in front of me.

In your vision, here, right close to me, you will have just my face and exposed armpits, white and dark hair in them, and the arms

73

and neck. My neck and arms. You stay in that space. I know that is all that you can see. My face. Exposed. Armpits.

Hair. Sweat.

Cunt is hot. It reaches right up through me and up to my heart and arms to where your fingers are still, sticking with our sweat, to my wrists. Left hand curling into itself beside you and brushing my leg, on the side of my calf. We stare a little longer. In your right hand you also have the cord.

You wipe your fingers off me.

Eyes still inside mine.

You pull the cord.

Pull it, a string right through me. A doll, I pose, hanging from it, relax and give in to the bracelets of pain around my wrists.

You stand, quick. Your heat and smell passes me. No breath in me as you pass. I crank a final look of my head to look up at you, right at you. By the time you have turned and begun to walk away, I am hanging whole body from arms above and opened right up for you to see.

Waiting for your gaze.

You move towards your seat. A line of shadow follows the very edge of your body. Light dazzles over the rest of your back, your legs and skull covered in skin and hair. The light pushes against the shadow line, as though it will push it off into the shadows that stay, undeveloping and seething in the corners of the room.

You pause before your chair. Left hand slightly behind thigh dances quick quivers between dazzle and shadow

Not blinking. The stinging and the light drips salty water out of my eyeballs. Cheeks wet. I imagine them, beautiful.

You turn and sit. Pick up your papers.

You draw quick, so quick. Your body is shuffling with the charcoal, covering pages quickly. Curving over your hand. Your eyes digging in. I hold the cord above me with my tethered wrists. Relax the rest of my body. A doll. Change poses less frequently. Wilt into each one. You cover many sheets, sometimes long sweeping arcs, your back pushing through them. Sometimes minute scribbles. Hunch body over and round your fingers as they tease out details. My details. Eyes flickering everywhere, glinting with the flecks of dust in the light.

Hot, hot my cunt is now. Feels the sparkling heat. Openness in the air. Lines curving all over me.

Sinews of muscles beating as they hang through me. My warm, sweat-flushed flesh hanging from the window. His lines curving all over me. My back arched with my arms. Legs hanging off, my head, fingers, open and slipping through this heat. Sinews of back, tense and pressing through at the bottom through my buttocks and in between my legs. The hair dripping. Dripping hair at the base of my neck. Drops fall cold, one, two, down the ladder of spine.

Don't shudder with the shock of the sweat falling. Arch and relax. He draws and draws and we stare and stare.

The piece of material is in his pocket, waiting. It is his handkerchief. He stands. The line of shadow a strip over his body again. My eyes in his eyes and his sparkling body coming closer.

His presence.

Breath heavy.
Heavy.
Quick and heaving flesh with sweat.

His eyes in my eyes again. Lurking shadows in small corners watch him come to me, do not grow.

Places the handkerchief over my eyes.

Summer white light gone, just like that.

Breath and heaving sweat are one thing in me.

He feeds a piece of the handkerchief around one side of my head with his fingers, stroking along my skull. He stretches the fingers around to the other side and slides the other piece of the handkerchief around. His fingers make a circle tight on crown of skull. Pressure. He brings the two pieces to the same point. Makes the knot.

His hand in my wet hair. Catching strands and pulling them.
Above me. Do not see him anymore. Just black. Sense him.
Each pull of the knotting moves my head.
Smell him. Breathe him. Heave.

Final adjustments to the blindfold. His finger moving
underneath it, on top of the skin of my forehead. Air quivering
near his left side. Against his moist fingertips are his dry
fingernails. Graze soft against my skin.

Sense him straighten himself. Stands. Breathes. Breathes hard.

Stands.
Hear him move away. Darkness moving in darkness.

Snug blindfold on head. Nose. Breathe fast. Hands above me
again. Tense body balancing. Bones of buttocks grind more into
the floor. Arms up, still tied. Breathe.
Relax.
Relax into each big breath.
Sweat-touched blindfold. Only material on my naked body.
Sounds of him sitting down.
Hear him settle back into working. Watching me. He has a
rhythm. Squeak chair. Pick up paper. Warp paper. Charcoals. I hear
every movement.
Posing is different now. Body has to think about balancing. Eyes
relax. They see stars in the blackness, the other senses work for
them.
That white heat is there, between my legs. Right deep in my cunt
now. Ringing through me. Ringing and hitting the base of my
spine. Spine extended and hanging, holding itself.
Holding itself and going up through shoulder blades and arms.
Letting the tied wrists hang off that same line of tension through
me.
Letting the body hang and balance.
Feet. Knees, buttocks.
Each change into pose, feel air and heat and rising sweat.

It all touches between my dripping legs. Wet.

Slip often on soles of feet. Roll and move into new poses. Fall between them. Smack of knees and buttocks on floor. Ankles crack. Let the pain ring through, right deep into spine and cunt. Keep posing. Breathe. Heave. Relax. Breathe.
Calm.
Calmness right through me. Don't even try, it is there. Right through me. Through the pain ringing and hitting. Through the breath that I suck in. The open feeling inside my cunt that blooms.
He draws and draws. Hear all of his movements

My skin slipping and sticking hot, feel the heat of the day, sweating me out. Its sun lights up with the stars inside the blindfold.
And stop.
Sheets of paper stop noise.
In out of lungs.

Hear him warp the paper, put it on the ground. The charcoals. Stand. Walks forward. Skin of my inner thighs electric static.
He does not walk to me.
Goes to his room.

In out of lungs.

He makes noises in his room.
Hear him open a cupboard door. Shuffling things. What is his left arm doing?
Dull thud. Shut cupboard door.
Feel darkness of the blindfold fall down over my body. Cold of sweat is a big shiver through me. Unregarded.

He returns.

Begins a few metres away.
Click.
Twist around. Expose my back. Knees crunch into the floor.

Click.

Sway my back into a sweeping curve, pushing buttocks into the air. Dangle my weight from my wrists. Relax my head down.

Body rocks, unbalanced.

Relax. Spread my knees out to steady myself. Click.

The light and the sweat heat come right back. Feel the dampness of the blindfold. Click.

See the sunlight through the pitch black.

My wrists beat. Weight traps blood in my hands. Throb in time with my skin, all over.

Click.

He moves quick around me.

Change my poses quick. On the sides of my thigh. Stretched up by cord. On my back. Bones remember the hard floor as they hit it. Bones in my buttocks, my heels, palms. Click. Lean back into arms. Bend my legs. Straighten. Extend and hold my spine. Click.

I hear his breath through mine. Each as quick as the other.

With the cord and the blindness and the camera, I open right up. Open and pose. Skin taut on my ribs,

I feel. Still air of the room over me. Sweat trickles. In out of lungs. His fingers flickering. Click. Imagine the lungs and ribs and legs and neck will split and open me further. As far as I can go.

I want to.

His breath heavy. Clicks quicker.

He comes closer. Feel him. Know what he is doing.

Coming closer.

I can hear his heartbeat beating with mine. Click.

He steps towards me. Click.

His legs are in front of me. I feel the heat and smell them. Lets go of the camera hanging around his neck.

His feet are inches from my wet thighs. His naked feet.

He has leant in. Feel that his hand is on the rope. The camera swings from around his neck into my forearms.

Our heartbeats strong, loud. I know I can hear them both.

He unthreads the knot. End of rope falls down, dangles. Touches my arms with the camera.

Sound of him running the cord again through the metal of the window pane.

He pulls it. Hard.

My wrists yanked up. Strain in wrists, elbows, shoulders.

Wrists hit the metal. Pulled up it.

Makes the knot. It is much higher than before. He almost pulls me from the ground.

Strain. Tightens my chest and lungs.

My stomach stretches with spine. Sweat unsticks my buttocks from the floor.

Taut.

Pulls. Harder. Unbalances me.

Arms and shoulders pull forwards and up. Head smacks back onto the windowpane.

Stars in the blindfold. Breathe.

Pain of skull hitting windowpane blooms and subsides.

Breathe deep again. Push weight forward onto my feet. Go to rise onto them, weight heavy in my thighs.

Tense buttocks, back, body.

Strain. Unbalanced. I push myself up. Feel relief on my shoulders and hands as weight moves.

His hand. Wet. On my shoulder. Our sweat mixes. His middle finger joints resting on the bones of my shoulder. Cupping them. Fingers hook under the shoulder blade ridge. He pushes down. Buttock bones hit back down onto floor. Head and shoulders smack window pane again.

Relax. Tell yourself to relax.

Click.

Stars. Ringing bright pain again.

Relax. I tell myself. Wrists beat with weight, constriction. Body swinging gently. Relax. Breathe through tension of stretched skin. Relax into it. Swing.

Succumb. Click.

Shoulders feel as though they could dislocate. Stretched, popping, from their joints. Breath shallow. Gasping. Pulls in and out of my throat, opens my mouth. Air hot. Mouth sticky dry. Click. His body still right there, in front of me. Hear him swallow.

79

Feel how close he is. In between my legs.

Ache.

Keep drawing in breaths. Rope cutting moist into wrist skin. Fingers thick and numb. Click.

Drop head back, crunches bones of neck. The pain of my head blooms and spreads down. It meets the hollow sick heat that spreads from my cunt to my stomach. It runs up my body in between the stretch sinews and spine.

Knees flopped open as buttocks barely touch floor. Feet sliding and wobbling, opening and waving bent legs. Click.

Click.

His feet slide further forward. His right foot raises. Slips under my bent leg. Slides silky quick up into the hot wet crease behind my knee joint. Stays there a moment. My lips make a moan. Secret skin of the knee crease slides against his.

Feel smoothness and cold of the top of his foot. He holds it there. Stuck with my moisture.

Slow I feel the hairs of his ankle, then material of his trousers, he drops his foot to the ground, slipping his leg against me, pushing. Let my leg open with his.

I want to drop all tension of my thigh. Let the thigh open wide. Easier with my weight resting on numb ankles. Knees falls further out than before.

Click.

He leaves his foot there, right beside my leg. Click. My other leg swings open. My buttocks push forward with my open legs.

Let my head fall further back. Touches the windowpane. Rests there.

Mouth slack open. Breath comes in out, whistling a little through my teeth.

He will see this. Look down on this, the darkness of my tongue and throat, sagging open. Natural tension in my hanging body. Slack muscles falling from line the tension makes. Down my arms and shoulders. Sweat that I feel down my cheeks and neck. Sweat that feels his breath, hot on it.

That is the image that he will capture.

Click.

His other foot comes forward. Wedges underneath me, right in between my legs. His trouser leg sticks to my cunt. Feel material soaking and sticking to it. My lips make a moan again. His leg real. Right there. Click.

Cold of his foot shivers me. It sits in the cleft of my buttocks. Click. Don't wince away. Skin soft with hair and anus all pucker up and away. Don't. Relax.

Hear me moan again.

Ice cold the contrast of heat of my cunt and his cool foot hard there.

Behind the blindfold the blood red of my eyelids. Click. Thick, it comes out of the black, rising.

Feel his upper body moving. His arm. Click. With each movement there is a click. He moves around, above me. Photographing many angles. Me from all angles. Click.

The silk white heat of my cunt spreads right in between to the top of his foot. Relax. Put my weight onto it. Click. My stomach leans slack off my spine. My breasts, off my ribs. My head, off my neck.

Feel that sickening pit of the beginning of coming.

His leg further presses into me. Click.

The clicking rhythm slows. Heat of the room and the sun and him. Beat of pulse in numb arms, beating with my breath, in out. Moan. His breath in. Out. Pushes his foot further in. I relax more against it.

Click.

His other foot moves away from my leg. Makes a little ice-rush of air.

As he moves it, I want it back. Want it back, touching my leg.

Beat of pulse is all the way through me. Coming from wrists, it lurches with my stomach and the coming feeling is a little closer. Whistle of air in my mouth. In. Out. Open. Dark. I know it is a dark hole, staring up at him. And him staring down. Watching me.

Click, a photo. His other leg moves. Unhook from my cleft. Sickening feeling drags.

A second. Two.

His breath moving his body. Racking it, like sobs. Fast, hot breath.

He moves quick.

He comes down.

Neat quick movement. His shins hit the floor. Hear bones smack floor.

He kneels.

Nubs of his knees push onto the inner skin of my thighs.

Right there in front of me. His knees touching my thighs.

I feel the sweat-cold sheen on my open thighs. Feel it blot on his knees, pushing there, back against him. Click. Soaking into him. My head down onto my chest.

I do not know if I am posing anymore.

His breath in my mouth now. Faster. Harder. Racking both of us.

His left arm shivers. Scratch of it against the floor. It is so close to my ankle.

Lurch of my between legs coming feeling. Inside me I am so hot. Hot like the unbearable sweat of a sweltering summer day. And outside it is that. Outside in this room. Feel it. Red dark of my eyes dances in my eyelids. Relax my ankle. Cave it towards his fingers.

Until touch.

There is touch of quiver fingers. His left fingers are there, trembling against me. Click. Moan again. His fingers tapping a beat, ragged quick on me. Up me. Lurch inside. Hot white.

Move my leg a fraction more. Into his moving fingers.

His right hand drops the camera. Hit of it against his breastbone.

A second. Two.

His right hand is free. Beside his leg, it drops and touches the floor.

He lifts it.

It touches me.

It is sticky on my inner soft thigh.

His palm touching and holding almost the entire piece of my thigh in it.

His skin. Muscles of his fingers. Fingertips. All firm and closed on it, on my white thigh skin. The fine hair, the soft, wet fat. Squeezing.

Our breath. Sweat pouring. His smell. My smell. Saliva I can smell. His knee is not in my cunt anymore. Wet and the hair there is ringing white with the lurching come feeling.

His hand tightens. Middle finger presses through the fat and into muscle. He holds. We breathe. Sweat. Quivering fingers of his left hand beat onto my ankle.

Pinch. His grip a vice on my thigh. Pinch hard. Feel his teeth clench. Pain runs down my leg. I succumb to it.

He holds more. I relax the fat and muscle into his hold.

His knee opens.

Relaxes his hand.

Gasp. I gasp. He leaves a memory of pain in the skin. He puts his knee against where his hand was. Lifts knee a little and presses. He catches my thigh skin underneath his knee.

His knee digs hard in between the muscle and fat.

He leans into me with it. Pushing my body more into the windowpane.

His hand quick on the blindfold. Pull it. Catches in my hair. Yank.

I don't gasp as my hair pulls out hard.

Light floods the dancing blood red of my eyelids. Light. White light in my eyes.

His eyes.

Him.

I see his eyes. My mouth open, breathing into him.

His eyes right open inside me, down through my ring wet throat and in the silky body, the organs all beating, right down there.

A swallow, his gaze, penetrating through entirely. I feel myself opening and splitting with the whites of his eyes,

a rip

and a cut of being entire visible, vulnerable to his eyes inside me.

They consume.

His hand quick again. Now beside my face.

His fingers near my mouth. Around my neck.

His thumb and index under jaw bone. Hold.

Squeeze through the sweat.

Tighter. Gasp in my throat pushes into my mouth but there is no sound of gasp.

Relax.

My legs pressed right open by his knee. Open cunt. Knee digs further into the muscle gap next to the bone of thigh. Open and dripping sticky mouth hole. Breathing hurts. His hand pushing on my windpipe. Barely lets air in.

His breath fast in and out and touching my face.

Feel his body weight behind his knee and hand. Pushes me with fingers. My spine into the windowpane. Each nub of back bone dug into.

Our breath. The only sound. I try to suck in and out.

Relax. Try to.

Completely succumb.

No sound. Blood fills my ears. His eyes. The light. The heat.

Inside, next to his knee my cunt throbbing in a time with breath. His knee slips on my dripping leg. Pressure gone. Second. Again. Knees me right up in the crease of inner thigh. All your weight. Pushing in between my legs. Material of trousers ripping at my skin as he twists his knee and hand gripping neck. The windowpane digging my back.

Throat throbbing under his fingers.

Stars in my eyes, where his face is. His eyes. Presses his fingers further around my neck. Tighter.

My breath stops working.

Between my legs, I explode. A sound comes out of my throat. A long hiss. It breaks the silence.

I am coming.

Feel the white light between my legs and through my body. In waves over me. Hissing. Choking. His breath and fingers. His weight. The beat of his right hand holding onto me. Come waves and waves and hiss. Everything stars and white. Bones of feet and buttocks and back and neck and skull and skin all together. All bloom.

Everything white.

I blink. I feel high. I can breathe.
His hand is still there. But I can breathe.
His eyes. Inside mine. Watching.
We watch.
We watch each other.
His grip slackens.
We breathe. We listen to our breath.
He blinks. I blink. My eyes were stinging dry.
His hand drops a little. The side of it rests on my clavicle.
My body is wet damp all over. Shudder of cold runs over it.

Our eyes drop to his left hand. It has slowed, no longer quivering. Instead, it is hypnotic. From the wrist it weaves, the hand loosely following.
. He pulls back from kneeling on my thigh. I wince a little inside. Does not show.
Deep breaths. Right to the bottom of my lungs.

We stare again. Breathe and listen to each other breathe.
We do not move for minutes.
Between my legs swollen with blood inside. My arms, beating to my numb hands.
Feet and back and skull all feel like fresh bruises. Fresh and ripe.
His eyes move away. He stands.

Above me, he unties me. His legs in front of me. His left hand still slowly swooping beside him. When he is finished, he turns. Walks back to his seat. He sits back into it.

He faces me and the window. His gaze looks above me and out.
I can no longer hear his breath. Or his pulse. It is quiet.

My arms come slow down past my face and are lying on my
thighs. Thick, heavy hands.

I look at them. They feel overstuffed at first. They want to burst.

Move my knees in together a little. Pulling my buttocks? bones
together on the floor.

Slow. I wait to feel my hands again.

I wait. Breathe.

Breathe and feel stiffness of posing. Of being tied up.
The hard surfaces.

Slow. Very slow. Get to my feet. Wince when I go onto my
knees. Wince comes out of my mouth. I do not hide it.

My spine does not want to unbend. My wrists do not want to
take my weight. Feet feel rigid. Body feels exhausted. I stand.
Blood rushes from my head. Concentrate on balance. Have to
concentrate and breathe for moments. Until my vision is there
again. My blood in my head again.

I look toward him. He is still looking past me. I turn to see.

Outside his window, the sky is a cloudless blue. There is no rain,
no threat of rain. Limitless blue. I can see the city. The whole
thing. The river. Trees lining the streets along it. The Kursall and
the bridges. The mixture of buildings, styles, colours. I can see the
ocean. The hill next to the beach. I can see no people, just the city.
It lolls down towards the ocean and then gives in to the endless
blue of it. Endless even as it meets the sky. Goes on and on.

We both watch them. They are so calm. So beautiful. Indifferent
to us, they go on and on.

Deep breath. I turn towards the room. In the corners, the shadows are stretched out in their sleep, thin and barely visible. He has taken up his notepad. He sketches, slow and thoughtful. I go to my clothes. Begin to put them on. He continues. When I am dressed he looks up. Stops sketching. Puts down his notepad and charcoal. Stands. He walks to his kitchen. Sound of a drawer opening. I turn again. The view is so vivid, so fresh. I want to lick it. Eat it. I see the glitter on the tiny waves, far out. Glitter fallen from the sun. He returns. Comes to stand next to me.

We look at each other again. I tilt my head to look up at him. We are about two feet apart.

Thank you.

As he speaks, he hands me an envelope.

Our fingers do not touch.

I take it.

I turn. Listen to each of my steps on the floor. Slow, clean sounds.

I leave.

I walk on the path next to the river. I squint because the sun is bright and I have no sunglasses. It is the afternoon; the heat at its most intense. The Spaniards at their most sleepy. I sweat, walk, squint. Smell the ocean river and watch it. See the fishes swimming upstream.

Stand and watch them. Brown-grey fish with faint spots. Some are as long as my elbow to outstretched fingers. They invert and revert their bodies from the stomach, in and out. In and out. They do not seem to move forward. They are in lines and small shoals, bending and unbending at the same pace.

When it is hot, the salt-fish flavour of the water is more acrid. It sweats, rots more in the air. Dog shit is shat out on the pavement and the grass and sometimes I catch the smell of that too. Next to the white, moss-stained bridge. White and faded elegance of the art deco patterns on it; there is a white fountain, made in the same style as the bridge. I listen to it and listen to the river beside it and the cars on the bridge, all at the same time. Sounds of flowing. Sweat breaks on my forehead. Soaks into my hair. Slowly, I feel it, spreading. Sit there and listen for a long time.

It feels like a long time.

Walk across the pavement. Decide to go down and underneath the subway. Cooler down here. No sun. Can see without squinting. There is usually a busker, but none now. Everybody sleeping. In between the filthy tiles there are neat, deep gaps. Almost trip on one. Tiles are all over the floor, the walls, the ceiling, all the same. Walk up and out of the subway and turn right. There is the hill to my left. The Tabakalera to my right. I see the building. Big and black eyed behind the wrought iron fence. Behind the trees. Green and lush and shading me, hiding the building. It crouches behind them, peeping at me as I walk past and watch it through the gaps in the leaves.

It waits for me. Black eyed and broken-windowed. And massive.

It waits behind the trees and I walk towards it and the gate. Staring black in the broad daylight.

And now, I am right there, at the gate. Huge and rusted and opened. The concrete driveway. The grass. More trees. The building. The big, open entrance. Its side draped with a huge, bright poster. Beside it a smaller banner. It is his exhibition. Eric.

Eric's exhibition. Say his name clear in my head. Repeat it. His exhibition.

I do not go through the gate. I look at the banner. The arrow next to it, pointing the visitors to the galleries where it is held. The entrance. The huge, bright poster. The building. The black eyes of the windows. The grass. The trees. The sleepy, bright, bright day. I look.

It feels like a long time.

He walks from where the arrows point. He is with another man and they are talking. The man beside him talks more, with Eric nodding and answering. See his mouth making one word answers. His left arm sways beside him. Loose, uninterested. The other man stops. Eric stops too and they turn to each other. They shake hands, loosely. They smile. The other man walks towards the main entrance. Disappears into it. When he is gone, Eric is left standing. He looks towards the gate. He sees me. We do not move. We watch each other. I do not move towards him. We blink. I feel my breath wanting to be quick, shallow. I hold it. He comes to me. With each step, I am holding his eyes in mine. When he is two feet away, he stops. His left arm carries on swaying at the wrist, as though he is still walking. We stand for a while longer. The day drifts past, around us, but we do not move.

Have you come to see the exhibition?

I reply, No.

His lips move slightly upwards at the sides. Slightly.

Are you in a hurry?

I suppose so. Yeah. I keep hold of the gaze tight.

Wait here. I have something for you.

He turns. I watch him walk away, in the direction of the arrows. Left hand sways quicker. He is not in a hurry. I lean on the gate. Quickly, he returns. In his hand is a large roll of paper. It is tied with string. He takes up my eye contact and we hold it again as he comes nearer. He holds out the roll as he takes his final step.

This is for you.

I hold out my hand. Do not touch his as I take it. Hold the roll beside me.

Thank you.

A long pause. When he speaks, the voice is quieter and sincere. *You're very welcome.*

I tilt my head. We carry on watching each other. I am aware that I have to leave, but I stay a while longer.

You were in a hurry? He breaks the silence.

Yeah. Yeah. I've got to go. I do not say that I am leaving the city. I leave it there, a fact, in the space between us. *Bye.*

Bye.

He begins to turn back towards the arrows. He pauses mid-turn and the left wrist and hand is leading a quick, loose sway by now. He turns back and looks at me. Into my eyes. I do not move at all. The pause lasts a moment. He turns completely and walks away. If he looks back, he will not see me. I turn and walk back towards the subway. The trees will block his view. I am gone.

In Inma's flat, there is no Bea. Inma has left. She was rushed, all noisy and stress. Her hug was quick but tight. A squeeze. child-height. She held and impinged on my breath for a moment and then looked up at me and said. *Gracias guapa, cuídate bien.* She gave me back my deposit. She handed it over in a white envelope on which she had written her phone number. I did not initially count the money in front of her, until she pointed at it and said, *Abrelo! abrelo!* So I opened it, counted the money. She looked satisfied. She told me to leave the key on the sideboard. And to keep in touch. She squeezed my arm and said one last, *Cuídate.* She left. I looked in my room. My bag. The roll of paper. A pile of stripped bed sheets. I won't see Inma again. I took the roll from beside the bag and went to Bea's room. Never. You think that you will see people again, but you never do. Bea's room. The door open, her few belongings scattered. A book. Her sheets slack on the mattress. The curtains shut, the light muted. I go towards the bed. Kneel on it. Lie on it, face down. Her pillow. Smells of her hair. Of her. Old smell. Push my face into the pillow and pull my breath in through it. Lie there for a while. Feel myself grow drowsy, comfortable. Roll over. Pull the sheets up and stand beside the bed. Replace the pillow. Bring the sheets up, fold the top of them taut over the pillow and tuck them in. Turn and open the curtains. Let the daylight in. The summer almost over by now, I can see it in the sky. Bea. I place the roll of paper that Eric gave me in the centre of the made bed. I walk towards the door, pick up the book, her hairbrush and put them on her side table. Bea, will I see you? Walk out, shut her door behind me. Pick up my bag. Leave my key on the sideboard. Set the lock to shut behind me, leave the flat. Leave the building.

Blink. Breathe. Breathe deep and fill my lungs. Feel them filling and full.

Outside, the world passes in a sun-glinting daze. I could be on a train, a car or a plane, the city flashing past, not fast but bright, overwhelming in its sunny brightness. It's so white, I cannot see. I blink and miss it. I blink and miss it and it's gone.

DEAD INK NEW VOICES

BRICK MOTHER
SJ BRADLEY

WILD INK
RICHARD SMYTH

CONTROLLER
SALLY ASHTON

WWW.DEADINKBOOKS.COM